T0110352

Beats of Loneliness & Other Stories

Misfit

PARTRIDGE

A Penguin Random House Company

Copyright © 2014 by Misfit.

ISBN: Softcover   978-1-4828-1899-4
              Ebook   978-1-4828-1898-7

All rights reserved. No part of this book may be used or reproduced by any means, graphic, electronic, or mechanical, including photocopying, recording, taping or by any information storage retrieval system without the written permission of the publisher except in the case of brief quotations embodied in critical articles and reviews.

Because of the dynamic nature of the Internet, any web addresses or links contained in this book may have changed since publication and may no longer be valid. The views expressed in this work are solely those of the author and do not necessarily reflect the views of the publisher, and the publisher hereby disclaims any responsibility for them.

This book is work of fiction. Resemblance to anyone, dead or alive, is just a coincidence. Names, characters, places, dates, figures and events mentioned in this book are either the product of the authors' imagination or used fictitious, and are intended for the entertainment purpose only.

To order additional copies of this book, contact
Partridge India
000 800 10062 62
www.partridgepublishing.com/india
orders.india@partridgepublishing.com

Contents

To my Parents
and Grandparents

Preface

The stories in this book were conceptualized when after my rigorous academic career I was suddenly introduced to an altogether different world that throbbed within the four walls of home. The inhabitants of this world, I observed, led a life that was far removed from the one led by those on the other side of these concrete structures that served as a boundary between the two worlds.

These stories are an attempt to lend a voice to the muted existence of this peculiar world with all its fears, concerns, hopes, obsessions and eccentricities.

The elements of nature surface in all the stories for the simple reason that nature is so closely bound to the spirit of solitude.

The stories echo the sentiments of those left out of the widely interconnected social fold. They showcase the life of those left far behind in the fast-paced caravan of life.

I hope my characters will strike a chord with my readers.

Author

A Word's Worth

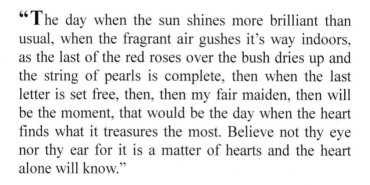

"The day when the sun shines more brilliant than usual, when the fragrant air gushes it's way indoors, as the last of the red roses over the bush dries up and the string of pearls is complete, then when the last letter is set free, then, then my fair maiden, then will be the moment, that would be the day when the heart finds what it treasures the most. Believe not thy eye nor thy ear for it is a matter of hearts and the heart alone will know."

"But?"

"You doubt?"

"If?"

"You trust not?"

"I do."

"Then leave and beware of the *silent observer* for he alone knows and knows too much!"

That was all that the oracle had to say.

Since then Saira had stopped listening to anything that granny had to say, any advice that granny had to give, any words of wisdom that granny had to impart. Saira instantly sat down to accomplish the Herculean task of setting the letters free though she spared a while to make sense of what it meant.

"Letters are to be set free. Hmm . . . and when the last letter is set free. But letters are what words are made of. So in a way I got to set free the words. Now how am I going to know which one's the last and whence it might be free?" she mumbled to herself, then glanced at granny who was busy knitting a sweater in her armchair.

"No," Saira decided, "granny would only drag the issue and discourage me." Saira decided not to tell granny anything about her plans.

"But which are the words that demand freedom? Umm . . . let me think." Saira closed her eyes and began to think. She heard something ringing in her head and instantly opened her eyes as if struck by an insight.

"Yes, it is his name and the letters that comprise it! And perhaps when I would scribble it down it would be set free from the bondage of my thoughts-my thoughts that keep his name forever chained in my memory." That day Saira sat down to scribble just one name on whichever paper she could lay her hands on. Even before the ink could dry over one page, she would be busy penning over another. Sometimes, in between when her slender fingers would refuse to go any further without a break, she would drag them to the margins of the page to doodle flowers and never forget to put a smile over each one of them-smiling, happy flowers. But she never allowed her fingers complete rest.

She soon discovered that ink and paper were not able to satiate the hunger of words to be drawn out-out in to the open where they could acquire their own identity. In fact charcoal was a better substitute and even better was ash from the fireplace.

"O Saira, my child! This is sheer madness. If destiny desires he would anyway be yours. And who ever knew what oracles really conveyed," and granny broke down in to sobs. Whole night her sobs rent the house with a gloom that no one sensed, for Saira was too busy scribbling to notice any plaintive note in the air though she heard the sobs. "O Granny, why don't you just rub balm over your nose and stop blowing it so hard?" Saira pitied poor granny for having fallen ill for an illness at her age could be really serious. Her long grey tresses, wrinkled skin, puckered lip, skeleton like hands with veins so prominent that Saira got scared even if she touched them by chance. It was a wonder how she managed to knit sweaters. Her fingers worked habitually, quickly and skillfully over the knitting needles. Going by her age she had probably not admired any of her works since a long time now.

Just one name all over the floor, over the curtains, over the walls, over the almirah, over the doors, over the windows, over the bedcover, over the pillows and over the bed itself. Granny's initial reaction was an obvious resentment for though she could not see the nuisance nevertheless she found the sniff of it unbearable. Wherever granny went the odour of coal had reached before her. But slowly the odour overpowered the olfactory and granny never sniffed anything unusual in the air of the house.

Each day Saira spared some time to observe the rosebush in her backyard. But the bush looked just the same with roses blooming and blushing each time the breeze jostled past.

"Testing times perhaps. I must not despair so soon," muttering this Saira set out on her daily routine of setting the letters free one by one, turn by turn. Having not spared even an inch of space with her writing, she was faced with the problem of space to set free the bonded. But the problem was after all not so insurmountable for she quickly realized the power of the scrubber with which she scrubbed away the old letters to make place for new ones. She would start early each morning with scrubbing of the floor and the walls and never end up writing and writing over and over again just one name, his name. She would write the name in bold letters shading the outline of each letter of the name over and over again till the inanimate letters were emboldened enough to come up alive in front of the observer. Observer? But there was no observer. Ostensibly there was one—the so called silent observer. In fact she wasted one full day looking for the *silent observer*. She looked in all the rooms, in each of the cupboards, under the furniture and amidst all that was capable of hiding someone behind it or below it or above it. But she found no one. Not a single soul. Perhaps the fault lay with her understanding of the oracle. Predictions have earned for themselves the bad reputation of being dicey after all. Nevertheless there was this one respite this time that granny had started showing an enormous amount of patience. She neither nagged nor stopped Saira from rummaging the entire house. Alas, greying years had taught granny to be calm and patient, thought Saira.

A few days later, while she was scrubbing the floor, Saira did find something that reinforced her faith in the oracle. She found a pearl, a real pearl, a pearl so white, so pure, just like the morning dew. She instantly threaded it and hung it on the wall and wondered how long it would take for the entire pearl-string to get completed. After this short pause, she resumed her ritual of writing. One by one she wrote the letters of the word, this time slowly-slowly for she began to think and thinking makes action slow. Why must she carry on henceforth? What if he did not return? What if he simply forgot? What if she had been already rubbed from his memory? "No, but the oracle predicted that the heart will find what it treasures most and anyway now I have spent a lot of effort in reaching thus far and now even granny endorses my stance, she complains no longer." And Saira began to doodle flowers on the floor. This time her flowers carried several whorls; petals over petals over petals. And when she lay back to admire her flowers she realized how horrifying they appeared. In her horror she even forgot to draw smiles over them. Unhappy, complex, dreadful flowers.

Letters that spelt his name, letters that spelt her feelings for him, letters that cried, "Set us free Saira! We want freedom." Letters that had been kept in confinement for who knows how long? At times Saira found that the letters almost flared up. Oh! They nearly burnt her fingers.

One quiet afternoon Saira noticed that the letters were mocking at her-teasing and deriding her for they were being set free but she was slowly becoming prisoner of her own thoughts, her own philosophy and her own daily rituals. Troubled thus, she stopped writing for a while and spent some time looking out at the deep red rose bush. What more could have delighted her than the fact that there were so few roses now blooming on the bush. "Good God! Just when would it completely dry up?" and she began to pray.

The *silent observer* watched. He watched Saira as she went about her daily ritual of cleaning, scrubbing and setting free the confined. He admired her dedication and her faith and her strong belief that her efforts would bear fruit one day. If only he was not silent. If only he had the power of speech; he could have at least complemented her. All the same, he did what he could best do. He watched and watched keenly.

That day, after Saira was done with her scrubbing, she looked at her hands as she was wiping them with a towel. Ugh! How ugly they appeared. Dry and worn out, they even had blisters and sores. She wondered what granny would think in case she noticed them for they looked more dreadful than even granny's hands. She rushed to her cupboard and picking up the bottle of moisturizing lotion sat down to apply it over her hands. She squeezed the bottle but the lotion did not flow out. She squeezed harder and a few solidified chunks landed on her palm. "I don't understand why these cosmetic companies can't make quality products," and she began to rub the chunks over her hands. It looked as if she had applied some adhesive over her hands. Unhappy with the result she began setting the letters free almost mechanically. The only remarkable thing that happened that day to bring a smile on her face was that she found some pearls that day. She instantly threaded them.

A few days later, as she was setting the letters free she noticed something very unusual about them. She noticed that the ones she was emancipating were crooked, bent and really hideous. They even moaned and grunted. So scared and baffled was she by the whole experience that her hands quivered as she attempted to liberate the bonded.

"What could it mean? Ha, but when are oracles so explicit?" she began racking her brain and in the meantime she began doodling crosses-cross over cross over cross. When she glanced at what she had sketched she realized it looked like a maze, the exit to which was nowhere in sight. On thinking hard she realized that the reason for the words to behave so strangely, to look so weird, was after all not so difficult to understand.

"Ah! They are among the last ones to be set free. Confined for so long under the heap of so many others, they have got their limbs broken, and now they moan and groan with the pain. What a long wait they must have waited! Oh! I can't believe this! So they are among the last ones to be set free," she spoke to herself.

Now when she scribbled, she found that the letters were turning more crooked and uglier with each passing day. She was thrilled-at long last the oracle was proving itself to be true.

One fine morning, she got up earlier than usual. In fact she had not been able to sleep peacefully the whole night for the moaning of letters had not stopped for a single moment. While she was scribbling after having scrubbed the entire house, she noticed that the sun was shining more brilliant than usual. Her heart skipped a beat. She rushed to her window to look at the rose bush. It was drooping and dry and all its red roses had withered away and all its leaves had crumpled. She could not have been happier. There was even a mild fragrance in the air. Even before she could collect herself there was a knock at the door.

"Hello! Is there anyone at home?" a handsome man could be seen knocking at the dusty door. With each knock dust fell on his neatly ironed coat. Each time he would wipe it off from his clothes with his handkerchief—his handkerchief that had the initials of his name embroidered over it. "Hello! I said hello!" he shouted but there was no response. Now he even began to cough as the dust spread in the air with each knocking. Tired of knocking and coughing, he was about to leave when the door creaked and scraped and opened making such a squeaky noise as if it had not been opened for ages. The opening of the door spread so much dust around that for a moment a film of haze engulfed the air. But a pair of sharp bright eyes probed, trying hard to look beyond the haze.

"Aha Granny! I am so delighted to see you! Is Saira at home?"

The old woman shook her head.

"No? I am already late for my flight. Hmm . . . okay when she's back just let her know that I kept my word, I came. Goodbye Granny! Aaa . . . and please ask someone to dust the door. B-bye."

The old woman waved at the man, still shaking her head. She kept waving at him till her eyesight did not allow her to see any farther. Then as if woken from a stupor she shut the door all of a sudden. She bolted the door. She bolted it fast and rushed to see herself in the mirror. And Saira saw a granny of herself in the mirror with a pearl string of exactly thirty-two pearls dangling from her wrist. The mirror observed. But it was silent.

Repair

House needs repairs. It asks for them. The leaking water pipes, the clogged drains, broken window panes, cracked furniture. If nothing else then there would still be door hinges which need oiling, else the door starts making squeaky, frightening sounds. Hinge-where the door is attached to the wall. Ignore the hinges and someday the entire door will detach from the wall. The house does need repairs. It asks for them.

Kartik was getting the porch repaired. Rains had played havoc with the floor. Mr. Sharma noticed this as he passed by.

"Getting your house repaired, Kartik. No doubt it remains in such good condition all the year round. The way you tend to your palms and crotons makes one feel that you are looking after your children. You know we keep watching from our balcony."

Now Kartik was beaming. Such compliments always gave him a great sense of satisfaction.

"Oh why don't you come in and have a cup of tea."

"No, thank you. Some other time." Mr. Sharma resumed his walk.

Kalpana looked out of the window. Kartik was still getting the work done. 'Oh, it must be tiring', she thought. She looked at the sky. It was overcast. Clouds, now grey, now almost black were rushing to every inch of the sky that filtered sunshine. She shut the window and came to sit on the sofa. She looked at the wall clock. Mohit was again late from college. And why should he not be? This time he was contesting the college elections for the post of secretary. Maybe she should take a walk in the garden and get a whiff of fresh air, she thought. She got up to pick her pink umbrella, then dropped the idea. She went in to lie on her bed. "Mohit isn't back. Hope he has not landed into a college brawl; hope he has not hurt himself," she kept murmuring to herself till she finally dozed off.

When and what woke her up, she did not know. But she opened her eyes to find darkness all around. She switched on her bedside lamp and found someone sleeping soundly beside her. She tried to recognize the man lying there fast asleep. Was it the same man she had got married to? Was it not possible that the man she saw off at the gate every morning did not return and in his place a man, a very different man came back home each evening? Wasn't it a stranger she opened the door to, every evening. But whoever he was he was very tired. As she recollected the day's events she rushed to Mohit's room. She felt relaxed on finding him asleep, a smile on his lips. Perhaps he was having a pleasant dream.

Entire house was at rest. Kamala's concern was the doors. Had they been bolted properly? Had any window been left open? Had the milk been kept back in the fridge? Had any jar been left uncovered . . . . At length she looked at the clock. It was the middle of the night. No, she could not ring up her friends at this hour. Supposing one of them rang her up. Still it would be a boring proposition for they would keep pouring their heart out and she would only manage a mere word or two of sympathy. Maybe she could turn on the T.V. but then T.V. made such loud noise and what if Mohit woke up. He would be cross. After all he had to attend to his college, studies, politics and all that. Maybe she should soak almonds for him.

Repairs went on for the entire next day. The chipping and scratching and polishing were irritating enough to confine Kalpana to her room for the whole day. She decided to use the opportunity to clear up the mess in her cupboard. There were clothes to be discarded, mothballs to be kept, saris to be ironed and what was this? A box hidden underneath the clothes? It was the jewellery box. She could not have been more careless. She placed the box on her bed and sitting beside it she opened it and took out her golden necklace, bangles and earrings one by one. She could not resist wearing them. The gold necklace pleaded her to let it adorn her fair neck. And the huge earrings, she held them in her hands. Their sparkle reflected in her eyes. She recalled when she had last worn her jewellery at a marriage party some time back. Make-up had failed to hide the envious looks on the faces of all other women at the gathering. She admired herself in the mirror and it only reassured all that she was already thinking.

Another day. Kartik had left for work. Mohit had his college to attend. Kalpana was alone at home, all alone. She looked at the walls, the ceiling, the furniture, the flower pots. There was no one else except herself in the house. If there was no one else then why did this nagging feeling never leave her that there was someone. Why was it that she became aware of its presence when all others had left and she was all alone in the house? Ghosts perhaps? But before purchasing the house they had enquired about the house and no one ever suggested it was haunted. In fact they had performed elaborate Havans at the house warming ceremony. She wondered whether it was plain oversensitivity of a woman given in to too much loneliness in a big house. Perhaps she should go out and check the mail-box. Perhaps not. After all who writes letters these days? Dumb chit chat over the phone, one liners through the e-mail, silly jokes over the SMS and cards to inform,'We have a happy/ sad occasion, reach at the given venue at given time in given dress-code.' But what disturbed Kalpana was why was she looking for an excuse to stay indoors? What charm did the four walls of the house hold for her that she did not wish to venture out?

The doorbell rang and Kalpana realized that it was already evening. She hurried to open the door for her husband. He looked at her in the face. She moved aside to let him in. "How was the day Kalpana?" he spoke firmly.

"The day?" Kalpana was left brooding over a question that demanded a quick, short reply, instant reply, a reply that is ready on the tip of the tongue. She wondered whether it was possible for her to sum up her experience of the day in words.

"And is Mohit at home or has already left to play cricket with his friends?" the husband carried on.

"Left," replied Kalpana.

"And what's cooking up for dinner tonight? Hope the tea's ready?"

"Ready," said Kalpana.

"And by the way, did the electrician turn up to repair the lights at the porch?" he asked. "No," replied Kalpana.

He left the room and she went on to make preparations for the evening tea. As she was going out she wondered how she had spent the day and how she could sum it up in quick one-liners. But why must she make an effort to sum it up in sentences at all, when her monosyllables were all that the world cared for.

You bulldoze a part of it or construct a new portion— the house never speaks up its mind whether it likes or dislikes, approves or disapproves the changes. So did Kalpana.

Another day. Yet another day. Same old day. Kalpana sat all alone looking at the walls. Walls that surrounded her. She kept staring at them for a while. They were made of bricks and mortar and painted on the inside in vibrant hues and embellished with paintings. "Yes, they resemble someone I have seen or met recently. Who could it be?" she murmured to herself. "Who could it be?" now she began thinking hard. "Strange, but don't they resemble me? The walls and I look so similar." And she recalled how she looked while she was admiring herself all decked up with her jewellery. Walls, they had been there ever since they shifted to the new house. Walls—they never seemed to have moved an inch. They never moved and did she? "Don't Kartik and Mohit come back to me each day as much as they come back to these walls?" she spoke to herself. She looked hard at the walls. No, there was no boundary left between the walls and her own self. Now she could easily cross over to the walls whenever she wished to. Deep inside the house a new world invited her. No, no norms, no pre-conditions. Joy that extended from infinity to infinity. No bondage, only freedom, emancipation. A world unknown. World where the day was not filled with empty hours but with love, unconditional love. The moment she closed her doors to the world of empty days, empty hours, empty minutes, this new world opened its arms to take her into its embrace. These were the moments when she felt one with the house; her persona synchronizing with the static walls of the house that may have never moved an inch but nevertheless were not lifeless either. And they always thought that house was a non-living entity. House that shared her loneliness, that shared the emptiness of her hours, that refused to leave her alone in the house even as others left to attempt to their worldly chores. How could the house be non-living?

Nature desires change and knows how to bring it about. If it is dull and drab in autumn, it will again cheer up brightly in spring. Time is the harbinger of change. What keeps count of time in a house is the clock. The clock ticks on. It must tick on. It was the wall clock that had incurred the wrath of Kartik. It had stopped all of a sudden.

"Kalpana, bring me the stool. Let me get the wretched thing off the wall. Clock stopping at the start of the day is not a good omen." Kalpana readily obeyed the commands. As Kartik fiddled with the still clock, Kalpana went into the kitchen to cook breakfast. The clock had stopped but the breakfast must reach the table on time.

By the time everyone sat at the breakfast table, Kartik was very satisfied with himself as he stared at the clock on the wall. "What a pleasure to be able to listen to its tick-tock once again. It livens up the room, doesn't it?" Others smiled in affirmation. Mohit ate his breakfast hurriedly and rushed to his motorbike. All that could be heard was the zooming of his bike. Few minutes later Kartik got ready to leave. Kalpana looked as Kartik waved at her. "Keep a close watch when the gardener comes to trim the hedge," he shouted. "Bye." Kalpana raised her hand, waved a little and then went in to clear the table. All her chores done, she sat on the sofa to relax.

It was evening and the gardener rang the bell. He liked working in this particular garden, for it was always taken great care of by the owner. Presently he saw Kartik coming. He bowed his head and Kartik reciprocated. Kartik knocked at the door. "Don't trim the hedge so short that it looks tonsured." Gardener observed the stern look on Kartik's face. Kartik knocked hard at the door. No reply. He called out Kalpana. Still there was no reply. "Kalpana must be in deep sleep." Both the men knocked harder still. No response. Kartik suddenly got concerned and asked the gardener to break open the door. Kartik rushed to Kalpana's room. She was not there. He checked in all the rooms. The gardener looked for her at the terrace, in the garden. Kalpana was nowhere to be found. Kartik checked on the telephone at all friends and relatives. No one knew where Kalpana went.

Mohit cried inconsolably as neighbours helped Kartik to a chair. Kartik sat on the chair, a lost man. Police was clueless to the whereabouts of Kalpana and puzzled still as no door or window was found open, no suicide note discovered, neither was any costly item missing from the house, the jewellery box lay intact in the cupboard, no cash was stolen either. Now friends and relatives and inquisitive passersby had started collecting at the house to offer condolences.

"Someone must have cast an evil eye," whispered someone.

"It was such a perfect house", a voice was heard.

"Oh! The weather is so depressing. It must have affected the woman's nerves," said another.

"Already, Kartik was telling me in the office that his wall clock had stopped in the morning—ill-ominous indeed," said Mr. Sharma.

The friends left, then the relatives. The soothsayers came when everyone had left. They examined the entire house, the walls, the ceiling and reached the conclusion that the house had an appetite of some sort.

When silence reigns, it reigns supreme. But the ticking of the clock breaks the silence of the house—clock that keeps count of time, of moments, of events.

Kartik was sitting in the lawn, impatiently looking at his watch first and then at the gate. He was waiting for someone. "Oh! I am glad you are on time," Kartik spoke suddenly getting up from his chair. He escorted the visitor to the door. It was the carpenter. "This is the door we broke open. It badly needs some fixing. Look at the hinges, they seriously need some oiling."

Home needs repairs but it is the house that manages to get them done.

The Wait

She was sitting on the porch, once in every while shifting her cane chair to remain in tandem with the traveling sun. But it was not for the love of the sun alone that she was there. The lone traveler of the sky unswervingly gave all the time he had to those who desired his company. It was Adil whom she doubted. Though for many years now Adil had lived up to her expectations, arriving sooner or later during the winter season, yet she doubted him. Suppose he did not turn up this season? She strained her ears to catch the faintest sound that spelt his arrival. Every now and then she would walk up to the gate as if her staying close to the gate would hasten his advent. Looking down the lane and not spotting him, she would get very disappointed.

Adil's entire family was busy packing his belongings for the journey. His daughter's fingers worked deftly and skillfully with the thread and needle embroidering the borders of shawls and adorning the necklines of suits with patterns and styles that were distinctly Kashmiri. Ouch! She pricked her finger. Lo, the artist inked her work. Assiduously crafting the paper mache boxes were his sons. When all was ready, the sons carried the heavy baggage over their shoulders and accompanied their father to the bus stand to see him off while his charming wife stood in her fenced garden, waving at Adil, with deep concern writ large over her face as if he was leaving for war.

"Shawl, Kashmiri shawl, suit, kesar, laung, akhrot!" The streets and lanes of the city reverberated with the crooning of Adil. His wares evenly balanced over the rented bicycle, as he peddled through the length and breadth of the city he longed to reach one destination in particular. He heaved a sigh of relief as he sighted the bespectacled octogenarian basking in the sun. "Shawl, Kashmiri shawl!" The three words were sufficient to make the old woman almost blush and hurriedly adjust her feet in her warm felt shoes. The wait was over. Adil was here once again. With him had landed Kashmir in its entirety, in all its splendor and beauty in the portico of the elderly woman.

"How's everyone at home Adil?" she queried the sharp featured, ruddy complexioned handsome fellow as he made himself comfortable in the adjoining chair.

"Fine, fine. I have managed a houseboat for my elder son and by next season I hope to marry off my daughter." Adil was pleased to be in the company of his most highly regarded client. She smiled and nodded and ordered her maid to prepare tea. She looked at him keenly through her thick glasses. Hmm, his looks had not undergone much change since the last year. Except for a few more strands of white hair, he looked quite the same. He was about twenty years her younger; perhaps more, were women more honest with revealing their ages.

"What's the specialty this winter?" Adil was only waiting to unbundle the package so securely fastened by his sons. "The stowls—plain, striped, or in jamawar style. These ones are in vogue. Your grand daughters will love them. The pashmina shawls, ah so fine and warm, you wouldn't require a sweater with them." With these words Adil started spreading out bit by bit of laboriously hand crafted magnificence of Firdaus's bar-rooh-e-zaminast (Firdaus's heaven on earth). The fine fabric fluttered in the air, making a wave and diffusing with it the subtle aroma of the paradise it came from before it settled layer after layer in front of her. The old woman's gloomy environs began pulsating with vibrant hues and patterns. As she stroked the fabric with her soft tender hands to feel the texture she sensed she had in some way touched the valley and the resplendent valley in reciprocation had touched her. The carved and painted jewellery cases, dry fruit boxes, wall hangings – there was room enough for all these and more in the old woman's trunks and almirahs where they would lay neatly stacked till her loved ones came over.

All the goodies in Adil's bundles were not hard to find in the suave and stylish malls and emporiums of the modern city all the year round. But with all their style and sophistication these malls were no match for Adil's superbmarket tied up in weather-beaten sheets. The personal touch with which he handled each of his customers was in stark contrast to the phony, well rehearsed 'Ma'am what can I do for you? Hello, thankyou, have a nice day,' of the salespeople, nay, the customer care executives and retail managers at the big shops. His concerns of the quality of his products and his marketing skills were not the synthetic mix of an unfeeling business enterprise. While thrusting himself body and soul into hard work, he had kept his soul free from the clutches of professionalism. His greetings were genuine and so were his concerns. His products were crafted remembering and recalling the sights and sounds of all those they were meant for.

This business season had proved to be quite rewarding for the diligent Kashmiri. Roaming the city streets on his bicycle he had managed to sell most of his stuff. For most of the city he passed off as a mere stranger but not for his cherished customers; the most treasured among these being the one waiting at the porch. Undeterred by the profuse bargaining by the matriarch whose wisdom of a lifetime had sharpened her skills of calculating the true worth of an object, Adil stopped over at her place quite often. It was both exhilarating and distressing when the season drew to a close. There was the thrill of going back to his family with his pockets full. There was the sorrow of parting from the old woman whose hospitality he enjoyed in the large city.

"Time to go back, Adil!" she sighed. "Your wife and children must be eagerly waiting for you."

"Yes, yes. Even my lamb will come bleating to me. And my daughter will hurdle the fence and rush up to me shouting, 'what have you got for me Abu, what have you got for me?"

"And what about the business season? Was it profitable?"

"Why, yes, with Allah's blessings and your good wishes it was indeed."

Today the old woman had made elaborate arrangements for the farewell tea party of Adil. There were sweets of various kinds, there was *Panjeeri made from pure desi ghee*, some of which she had packed for him to take along. Both of them were sipping and enjoying their last cup of tea together, for this winter at least, when Adil's face suddenly tightened up with a seriousness so unlike his jolly expression.

"Hope you wouldn't mind if I said something which perhaps I should not be saying." The grand old woman looked at Adil with surprise. He had never sounded so mysterious ever, all these years that she had known him.

"What is it Adil?" she spoke, her voice marked with apprehension.

"It is a fear, a constant fear. Each year before I come to your place I get anxious not being quite sure of finding you alive on my arrival." His voice shaking, Adil somehow managed to complete his sentence.

The frowns over the wrinkled visage deepened. She was old, reasonably old by any standards. Every winter she wondered whether she would manage to give death a slip and enter the New Year hale and hearty. Every season that she managed to survive was a bonus for her. She braved these fears each day to sail in to the next one. But wording these fears and bringing them up for a conversation – alas, her bravery did not allow her that. She turned her face away from Adil, having nothing to speak on a topic she was most uneasy with. Adil took leave of her in a most unceremonial of farewells she had ever given him. Mounting his bicycle he pedaled away without looking back even once. For a long time even she was not aware of his absence. Who could know if this parting was for ever and ever? Who could tell if those who parted here would ever meet, in this world or the next? Who could?

A year had lapsed. It was winter again. The lone traveler of the sky was once again busy doling out his blankets of warmth to all those who could afford to pay and to all those who could not. There was the porch with cane chairs neatly arranged in a semi circle. But the old woman whose presence adorned the porch was not alone today. Her grandson had come to spend the winter with his loving granny. He was busy reading out the morning paper to her. Starting from his favourite section on sports and carrying on through the page on cinema to some local news, shuffling the crispy paper he returned to the headlines on the front page, reminding her of the times when his grandpa used to read out the paper to her. She reclined in her chair, evidently quite delighted at whatever was being read out to her. But it was not the content of what was being read out to her that brought her joy. Rather it was the magic of the whole situation—the voice of his grandson, his sitting so close to her, the feeling of being loved and cared for—that made her face glow with happiness. She was sitting, warm and cosy in her chair, once in a while gazing through the bars of the gate to see if Adil was coming.

"Kashmir! Now listen granny here's some news about the place Adil comes from." The reference of Kashmir made her cheeks rosier still. She looked intently at him but he was quiet.

"What is it now, wouldn't you tell me?"

"The news is not good granny. Kashmir was rocked by an earthquake yesterday. Several have died. Some of the survivors are still trapped in the debris. The situation is grim."

"Wahe Guru, Satnam, Wahe Guru!" The wrinkled face at once became pale with the shocking news. Her grandson could sense the anxiety gripping her.

"Have faith granny, not everyone was affected. Perhaps he was one of those lucky ones."

The woman became quiet and still. Her eyes were now fixed at the iron—gate. But she could see no one across it and she could hear no one beyond it. In the evening when the maid came over to switch the lights on she found the old woman still sitting at the porch staring into the darkness.

Days passed but Adil did not come. The aged woman's heart was sent pounding with the slightest sounds coming from afar. But she would soon get disappointed on discovering it to be some other Kashmiris selling shawls or just some vegetable vendors. If everything was alright and nothing had gone amiss then why was Adil not here? By this time he ought to have arrived with his bags all loaded, happy and cheerful. The follow up of the news by her grandson brought no consolation to her. She started spending more time praying and reading the Holy Scriptures. But there was no peace still. Even the lone traveler of the sky was getting harsher by the day so that now it was not feasible to sit in his presence the whole day long. This was an additional cause for worry, for her wait was hooked to the gate outside.

It was one of those more warm days when the old woman dozed off sitting over her comfortable chair, while at some distance from her her grandson lay relaxing, his face covered with the morning paper to keep away the sunlight. "Shawl, Kashmiri shawl!" The lounging duo paid no heed to the voice. "Shawl, Kashmiri shawl!" the aged woman still reluctant to spoil her nap called out to her maid to ask the Kashmiri fellow to leave. "And tell him I already have a huge collection of all that these boys sell" she spoke while still half asleep. The maid rushed out to obey the commands. "Adil Shawl Wala!" the Kashmiri shouted. The old woman was shaken instantly out of her sleep. Rubbing her eyes, she adjusted her spectacles over the bridge of her nose. Fainter then faint then clear then clearer, right in front of her eyes emerged the handsome figure of Adil. Without bothering for her felt shoes she ran forward to hold and touch him to know if it was all real.

"Oh Adil, you are back!"

"Of course I had to. It just got late because the roof of my barn caved in because of the earthquake, ah, you must have read in the papers. My sons and I not only repaired it but also helped the other fellows in need."

"Look you always kept worrying whether or not you would find me alive on returning in winters but this time round you had me worrying for you. It was I who wondered whether or not I'll find you alive this winter season."

With the same hurry that the maid had rushed out, she now rushed in to make preparations for the welcome tea party.

"See granny I told you he would be back, now didn't I!"

"Adil would come even with a bullet pierced through his heart!" With these words of Adil, Kashmir once again descended at the porch of the old woman with the promise of staying there for the rest of the winter.

Beats of Loneliness

He was hurrying through the narrow lanes of the village with children following him at close heels. Banto was busy pasting dung cakes on the wall for drying when she noticed him coming from the opposite direction. She kept her gaze fixed at him till he had not moved out of sight. "It is going to be an auspicious day indeed," she smiled and said to herself. He moved on, following the tracks of good news. Tracking good news was his job. Jaswant, the drummer, who encased the spirit of Holi, Baisakhi, Diwali and many other festivals in the hollow of his drum, letting them out at the right moment with skills that had remained unchallenged. If you were ever to ask any stray dog in the village about his address, the dog was sure to lead you right up to his house-so they said. Laadi was resting on her charpoy when she noticed him pass by. She instantly instructed her daughter to immediately stop chopping the fodder for the cattle and follow Jaswant and run back home to report to her without stopping even to exhale her breath. After all Laddi must get her facts right before she passed them on to other women; the world wise web of women in the village that kept the information highways of the village running smoothly.

"A son at Bansi's," reported the girl panting for breath.

"A son then, huh, why, I should have guessed that. They don't beat drums for daughters," said the mother laying back on her charpoy.

Yet another day saw Jaswant tying his Kullewalli turban and donning his neatly ironed dhoti kurta complemented with a beaded jacket. His dhol slung across his shoulder he was about to leave when Bebe intercepted him in the verandah.

"Where to Jassa?"

"To Lambardar's"

"Lambardar's? All marriageable ones already married and no woman expecting as far as I can remember, what are you going for at the Lambardar's?"

"Lambardar's Mother. She died."

"She died! When?"

"This morning."

"Oh! May god bless her soul. Her last rites indeed need to be performed with beating of drums. She lived to see her line prosper to more than two generations. How many are fortunate enough to live such long?"

"Now if you have finished, can I leave?"

"Oh yes, why not," Bebe replied smoking from her hookah and staring at the farthest object she could set her eyes on. Smoking was a constant companion to Bebe just as the dhol was to her son. They prefer to call this world as the Karmabhoomi-the world of action—even when there is so much more time than is required to indulge in Karma, in action. But beings have been wise enough to fill these vacant hours with seemingly useless activities; activities which on repeated performance help to assign some meaning to the otherwise meaningless empty hours. When they lead to elevations they call them hobbies and when they lead to depressions they call them addictive bad habits when both are attempts at implying more meaning to life than the Karma theory assigns. What did Bebe actually smoke? Tobacco? Her lungs? Her worries? Time? Whatever! But she had indeed found a companion that broke in to the silence zone of a lonely widow with its hubble and bubble.

"Aren't you home early today? What all happened at the Lambardar's? Tell me everything in detail." Bebe said excitedly as she waited for her son to narrate the day's happenings to her. But Jaswant did not reply. He dumped his drum on the floor and straightaway headed to go to the back of the house. Back of the house was a stretch of some measure with trees, plants, shrubs and a shed that housed unused articles—broken pieces of furniture, old rusting iron articles, empty cardboard boxes. Things that the house did not require had been pushed to the back much like the thoughts that Jaswant was trying unsuccessfully to push to the back of his mind. How long does it take for such disturbing thoughts to shift from the conscious to the unconscious. While the unconscious dares you in dreams and Freudian slips, there is no escape from the conscious thoughts that flood the mind, inundating the self. They haunt you in the day, they will follow you to your bed, they will stalk you as you try to sleep and then they will masquerade in your dreams as you try helplessly to identify the characters. Jaswant went into the shed and rummaged the articles looking frantically for nothing. Nevertheless he found. He found a crude garden tool and started digging the flower beds. He dug and he dug. He dug out the dry drooping ones as he did some fresh ones. All of a sudden he dropped the crude item only to pick up a broom. He started gathering the dead dry leaves with the broom. But there weren't many. He had only gathered them yesterday and dumped them in the pit. If only the broom could cleanse the mind of its disturbing thoughts. All this while Jaswant kept murmuring something to himself. While sweeping he went too close to the young kittens yawning and rolling in the grass. They noticed Jaswant but kept rolling. Jaswant was a familiar face with the kittens, they need not fear him. Their mother trusted their custody to the secluded spot in Jaswant's backyard, but today Jaswant wanted to sweep just the spot where the kitties lay lounging.

As the spiky thing in the hands of the sulking man came close then closer, the tender white bundles of fur ran for cover farther and farther away. If a man could peel the layer of grass from the ground he would definitely have been Jaswant that day. Nature heals and embalms the distracted minds but only if someone would leave the broom and stop sniffing the rising dust-for there are subtler fragrances in nature's fold. The sulk thought it was time to retrace his footsteps from the backyard and dropped the broom. He turned to move away, then stopped and looked around. Bebe could hear him remove clothes from the wash line. His pulling at each cloth, the swiveling and rattling of pegs on the wire interfered with the usual hubbling bubbling sounds that Bebe was used to hearing the whole day over.

"Why, what happened Jassa?" asked the mother as she heard him placing the clothes on the charpoy.

"I met her on the way," he shouted.

"Who? Her? My God! What is she back now for?"

"She's asking for some money."

"Did you say money? But haven't we given her a lot already!"

"She says she needs to go to the doctor."

"What for?"

"Her wounds."

"Wounds again? Haven't they healed? Never heard of a woman like her. When on earth did women require doctors and healing. What would other women say if they ever heard of it?"

"What are you saying Bebe?"

"I am speaking the truth. I have been a woman all my life, don't I know that suffering a while alleviates all aches and pains of women. When did women require doctors? When did they require treatments?"

"Bebe she was crying in pain?'

Bebe was quiet for a while then thinking something spoke. "Okay. I'll give you the money but take me to the kitchen first for I'll boil a concoction of tulsi and ginger and other herbs. It surely will cure her. Take me there quick. You know my eyes, they don't see the world as they used to."

Jaswant led her to the kitchen, lighted the fire at the chulha and put the vessel full of water over it as the old woman kept instructing him the quantities of all the ingredients. She squatted on the floor as Jaswant stood anxiously watching the herbs simmer in the water.

"Jassa, what was she wearing?" the old woman spoke out all of a sudden.

"The same red salwar—kammez, mother."

"The same? Is it bright still or has the colour of her suit faded?"

"I did not notice mother? But why do you ask?"

"I ask because I think it must have. Much like the world that I see now with colours fading, lights growing dimmer, shapes going awry and all forms melting into one another."

Jassa did not speak. He kept his gaze fixed on the simmering liquid in the vessel. When this gazing sucked all patience out of him, he began pouring the concoction in a glass bottle.

"Seal the bottle tightly and tell her to take small sips from the bottle." Bebe spoke facing the direction of heat and smoke emanating from the chulha. Jassa had already left in hurry.

Solitary Jaswant headed straight to the secluded green patch just outside the village right to the bottom of a dried up well to spend yet another lonely evening. He climbed down the dreamy steps that led to the interior of the well that once was capable of quenching the thirst of parched souls. One place where Jaswant was allowed to be himself once again. One place where he and she had woven and spun dreams of their future life and she had even dyed them in vibrant hues. One place where they had together played hide and seek. One place where she now played hide and seek with him. Now, several years after her death whence flouting all the rules of the game she had gone into permanent hiding making only brief whimsical appearances.

Today he was all alone in the well. She had not arrived. Whether she would come at all was hard to tell. It must be real difficult to cross over from the other world to his own, he thought. He wondered whether Yam's guards would grant her permission today or not—for there must be so many of them wanting to cross over from the other world to this one. But he could wait. In fact he loved waiting for her here in the cool interiors of the dried up well. It was getting dark and there was no sign of her coming. He could leave the message with the well he thought. In fact he had done this on several occasions before and the well had most sincerely conveyed the message.

"Here, here is the money, this bottle and here give her this bundle as well." Tears rolling down his cheeks he took out a bundle of sweets from the pocket of his beaded jacket. He started crying bitterly and his cries struck against the walls of the well and kept falling down till they were depleted of any energy to strike again.

Cool breeze was blowing accompanied by sweet fragrance of flowers when it noticed the drummer sitting alone and sobbing.

"Shouldn't we stop here a while," it asked the fragrance.

"But we still have a long way to travel, we cannot afford to stop," replied the fragrance.

"Can't we help him in easing his sorrow?" again enquired the breeze.

"Men, men! When could their sorrows be eased? It would be a sheer waste of time and energy," fragrance said tersely.

"Perhaps we could ask the stars to help him," said the breeze with a look of concern in her eyes.

"Umm, good proposition." the fragrance said thoughtfully. The kind duo, the merciful duo spared a moment to plead to the stars for help and after a moment went on its way.

"Which one were they referring to?" said the brightest star to the one next to him. "I can't say they all look the same from such long distance-mere specks. Okay, let me see. I think it's the one inside the well." The star replied scrutinizing the earth below.

"Lets dim our lights tonight!" suggested the brightest one.

"Why dim?" questioned the less bright.

"Men prefer it dim in sorrow," replied the brightest.

"Who told you that?" queried the less bright.

"I have been observing it through the ages," said the brightest one.

"Ah observation! But you are forgetting something my dear."

"What?"

"Today we have to attend the party at the Moon's. We can't afford to dim ourselves tonight. No, not tonight."

"Well then, let's let the earth solve her problems for herself."

Jaswant climbed up the steps of the well wiping the tears with the sleeves of his kurta. By the time he reached home Bebe was already snoring on her charpoy. Jaswant made his way to his bed in dark, hoping to sleep away the torment of his life.

He kept tossing on the bed, pulling the sheet and tugging it under his feet. His mumblings and coughing broke the silence of the night every now and then. He kept fidgeting, and now even the bed started complaining. It creaked and cracked and cursed the sleeper. It was some time before the bed could rest in peace. Jaswant woke up suddenly as if frightened by a scary dream. He started pulling at the sheets again and the bed realized that this man was not worthy of receiving its warmth. He scanned the bed in the darkness of the night and realized that it was too large for him or rather he was too inadequate for the bed.

He turned on it then got up and switched on the light to check what hour it was that did not allow him a wink of sleep. Then he looked across the bed. There was a pillow on the other side. He almost saw his wife's beautiful and serene head resting over it. He rubbed his eyes and on closer examination actually found a long strand of hair lying on the pillow. He switched off the light and lay down on the bed. He shut his eyes and once again the drowsy intoxicated faces of drunken men encountered him. The faces kept dancing around him. The sound of the dhol kept drumming hard on his tympanum just the way he beat the stretched membrane of the drum.

Now he realized how painful the drumming must have always been for the drum. How ruthless he had been, how merciless, to beat someone so hard. But the drum looked quite inanimate hanging on the peg over the wall. Then why did it make so much noise on being hit. How could it have never occurred to him before? He had been aggressing against the drum all his life and the drum had always borne his aggression without complaining even once. But was the drum a separate identity? Wasn't it one of his own vital organs? Had he not been beating his self since the day he parted from her? What a relief it was being one with the cathartic drum. What faces were those that surrounded him? Who were they? He tried to identify them but could not. Every day a new occasion, every day some new faces that jumped and hopped and danced all around him. What dance was it that they danced together when their dancing and his drumming were not rooted in the same emotion?

The fragrant breeze was happy at accomplishing the distance it had set out to cover. Twinkling stars were happier shining so scintillating, so bright at the party.

Karan Karan

❧

"Karan! Karan! Are you coming? We are waiting here for you!" Rani quickly woke up from her nap at the huge sofa. Waking up thus, late every afternoon, was becoming more of a habit with her. Ever since she had shifted to the new neighborhood she had been shaken out of sleep by the same shouting and yelling of children on their way to the play-ground, calling their friend Karan to join in, every day at the same hour. Rani looked at the clock and smiled. They might be late for school and homework but when it came to play, children could impress by their punctuality.

Rani went into the kitchen to make herself a cup of tea before she geared up for some household chores—if a term could be borrowed from the regular homes for a single working woman staying alone in a city . This was the time, these were the hours, she had entirely to herself. In a few hours she would sit down at her system, check her mails, answer some, delete several and try to catch up on what had been going on in her absence in the office. She could not afford to neglect the goings-on of the place she would inevitably have to go back to at the end of the summer-break. Then life would be different. Then she would don her gibberish self, play her social roles. But in these empty hours of her holidays she had all the freedom to be herself, sitting quietly and peacefully all by her self, thinking and doing what she liked, the way she liked, without any interference, or sometimes not doing or thinking anything at all, just being content with being a part of the moment itself. Having made hardly any acquaintances in the new neighborhood, spared her the torment of endless meaningless conversations.

"So, was Karan on time for play?" It was the first question that Rani's mother asked each time she called her up at the appointed hour every evening. Rani's pleasant replies to such queries comforted her mother immensely and mitigated, if for a while, the apprehensions of a mother whose daughter had resolved to build a career for herself even if it meant staying far away from her family. For Rani, too, there was a contentment in these seemingly small talks. They conveyed to her that she still belonged to the family and there were those who cared for what she did and how she spent her days. "In fact the television serial 'Mahabharata' is also telecasting the episodes related with the life of the mythical hero and son of the sun-god 'Karan' born to an unwed Kunti," Rani's mother would go on, attempting to find some common ground for conversing with her daughter.

Summers were at their peak, so that now there always seemed more time that needed spending in the empty hours. The sweltering heat also had its sleep inducing effects when it sapped all energy forcing one to droop down. But this lullaby effect of summer had failed to hold its sway over the young ones who were in time for play with renewed enthusiasm. Today Rani woke up to a slightly different note. As she rubbed her eyes and strained her ears to hear, she found out that Karan had perhaps bought a new bike that the rest were pestering him to get along and also allow them to ride. Rani ambled her way to the balcony to have a look at the new bike. But the energetic zealots had already left. She stared at the empty street. The sun was still blazing and the sight of a stray canine dozing under the shade of a tree sent Rani back to the couch. So that when her mobile rang in the evening her ringtone kept playing its full versions giving the impression of someone listening to their favourite number. "Lazy Rani! What was Karan upto this afternoon?"A very concerned mother addressed a daughter still in sleep. "Today, today well, he had bought a new bike." Rani spoke drowsily. The reply did little to assuage the unease of a mother whose young pretty daughter lived all alone in an unfamiliar city.

Since it was going to be yet another sultry day, Rani had already chalked out her plan for the day to break the monotony of her routine. She had decided to tidy up the kitchen shelves and hang some really dark shaded curtains to keep the sun at bay. Keeping the sun away was not as simple as she had thought. Its potent rays managed to work their way in to the rooms. She was up the whole morning running around, adjusting the cooling systems, plugging the gaps in the curtains, drinking iced beverages, bathing more than usual, trying to evade the power of the sun but by afternoon she decided to give up. In this battle that nature waged against the mortals, the one in shining armour had once again emerged victorious. The heat of the victor burned everything that offered resistance. Rani paid the price by abandoning everything else for the love of a nap. The touch of sun, its sizzling embrace allowed no room for any other thoughts. Willingly or unwillingly Rani was forced to sacrifice herself at the altar of the blazing god.

"Karan Karan! Get your cricket bat. Look we've got a new shiny red ball. Hurry up now Karan we are already late." It was again the shrill shouts of Karan's friends that shook Rani out of her sleep. As she was getting up, she heard her mobile ring. It was her young nephew calling.

"Mama says I need to finish my holiday homework first. After that we will come to your place."

"Yes indeed."

"How's Karan? Does his mama also tell him to finish his holiday homework?"

"Oh yes, yes why not?"

"When I come will Karan play with me?"

"He would love to Sanju, he'd love to."

"Say my hi to Karan and bye-bye."

"B-bye and take care."

Rani hurried back to tidy the place realizing she was going to have visitors for the summers. As she was doing so she peeped through the windows. No, she could not see them playing but she could hear their distant voices as they played cricket. 'Karan must be the ring leader or else why would the other children flock to his place and not proceed further without him,' Rani surmised. She was reminded of her own childhood when she was bullied over by the big girls in the group. Oh how much she detested those moments. But Karan was not the one to allow being intimidated. Karan—without whom the team was not complete. Karan—whom the others pleaded to join them. Karan—who kept them waiting at his door. Karan—whose name rent the air each late afternoon. Karan—the hero, Karan—the champion.

Summer showed no signs of relenting. Lazy days, idle days, moving at a sluggish pace. Rani was trying a new dish, fuming with the fumes going up in the kitchen when she heard the doorbell ring. She turned off the gas knob and went to answer it wondering who it could be at this hour at midday. She opened the door to two visitors, complete strangers. The amiable woman introduced herself as her neighbour. Before the young lad beside her had the chance of introducing himself, Rani gave out a loud cry, "Karan!"

"No, that's my son Tinni. Tinni say hello to your aunt." The woman spoke as her son shied away behind her. Rani led her uninvited guests in.

"I wanted to pay you a visit earlier but couldn't make it so today when I found some time I took the opportunity to come over."

"That's very kind of you." Rani smiled.

"You and just you? No husband and children ?"

"No?"

Rani smiled again though this time it was a forced one for she realized that she was slowly foraying into the zone of idle talk. She quickly sneaked into the kitchen to get some eatables for her guests. As she offered them to Tinni she sat down beside him.

"Do you also play with Karan?" The child stared at her blank faced chewing a mouthful of the candies, showing his broken milk teeth. A disgusted Rani turned her face away. 'Karan would never befriend such a dim-wit,' Rani thought. She turned her attention to his mother.

"Your son also goes out to play with the other children." She enquired.

"My son, no my son plays at home. Oh he has such a huge collection of video games and toys. Come on over sometime and I'll show it to you."

"No, no that's alright. But don't you think children ought to play outdoors to build strength and enjoy themselves?"

"My son is very smart at the games, aa video games. You must come over to my place to see that."

"Yes that's all right but you should send him at least sometimes to play outside with the other children when they all go out together late in the afternoons."

"Did you mention other children? But all those people who live around in the neighborhood have only grown up children, nay adolescents, who are always nose down in their books." The woman replied patting her son fondly over his back.

The conception of Karan in a sunny embrace had taken place yet again.

Mast Yogi

Neeraj was glum. His face carried the expression that you would expect on the face of a young man who has just finished shuffling the pages of an employment journal. The journal that suddenly makes one realize that one is a little less educated, a little less professionally qualified, a little less experienced, a little less capable, a little less worthy of deserving a good life in a big city. City, that never remains idle. City that never lets anyone remain idle. What use was the journal after it had been read? And what use were his degrees neatly placed in the file? Oh, why had he worked so hard to obtain them? This side of the road did not have any opportunities for him. Were there any across the road? When opportunities cease to knock at the door then one must gear up to explore them and drop one's resume with them in case they feel like knocking again; they should at least have your latest whereabouts.

Neeraj looked at the road that he was to cross. But the road was not quite discernible. Automobiles had flooded every inch of it. He could just about make out a divider ahead, and another road still further that enabled the one way flow of the traffic. Automobiles whizzed past at amazing speeds. Oh it made him dizzy. The pace at which the city moved was nauseating. Nauseating? But perhaps for the one who stands stationary by the side of the road.

Neeraj managed to cross the road. Standing at the divider he ran a quick glance at the tall buildings on the other side. Who would believe they had been built by men nearly his own height when they dwarfed men to sizes where living men became worthless while lifeless buildings kept appreciating in value. He turned his gaze closer to his shoes and the grass he was trampling. At some distance Neeraj noticed him. But he could not hold Neeraj's attention for long, for Neeraj longed to cross the road, to move to the other side, the other side that was lined with tall buildings. He was not interested in Neeraj either. He kept sitting, facing the traffic and at the same time turning his back to it. Entire city rushed past at varying velocities in one direction at his front and in the reverse direction at his back so that the sum total might be assumed to be a zero—round and perfect.

He sat there ruminating. His head high, his expression somber, gazing neither at the traffic, listening nor to the unnecessary sounds it made. One humped bull, the black of his skin merging with the earthy brown, with short dark horns—all alone sat the Yogi in deep meditation as if on the banks of two rivers; the flow of one contradicting that of the other.

The flow stopped for a while. Sirens blared all around. Neeraj rushed inside the nearest building he could; his life instinct having struck an association with decibels. Entire area was cordoned off. City halted but did not lay idle. The protesters were demanding clean drinking water. The traffic waited with baited breath to let the Demonstration pass by peacefully. While men panicked, men in uniform scampered around to control the panic. Ambulances kept screaming at some distance

The demonstrators voiced their demands, full throttle. They wanted a quick solution to the problem of shortage of clean drinking water. So, water had after all not remained water, it had become a problem that needed fixing. The Yogi kept ruminating tranquilly. The high pitched drama had no relevance for him. He was not thirsty for the present; the prospect of getting thirsty was not something that could bother him. The madness of the city could not affect the one who drew his nourishment and not his existence from it.

The city resumed its pace. The flow of traffic became smoother through the pipe-like roads. The Yogi sat meditating over the beauty of being. Being that is not the same as dwelling for in dwelling one often gets stuck up. Vehicles whizzed past, hurrying and honking.

It was evening and Neeraj again confronted two roads and a divider. He was tired. His lips were dry. He looked around for a source to quench his thirst. At some distance a water-pipe had burst open. Bursting open is natural when pressure exceeds endurance limits. Scores of bipedal were already crowding the spot with buckets and cans. Neeraj hoped to get a few sips before resuming his journey and so did the Yogi.

Living in the big crowded city had made Neeraj learn the tactics of wading his way through to attain the attainable.

Water was clean. It was cool. Neeraj quenched his thirst. The Yogi tried to negotiate his way to the water source but could not. He watched the bipeds push, pull and jostle around. He chose to go back to the green patch. They were far more impoverished than he had thought.

He sat down in silence all alone in the midst of the racing city. Endurance limits of the patch overhead had expired. The Yogi got what it needed and got it effortlessly.

Veil

And who says that in this world joys and sorrows are balanced. Indeed if they were, we would all be neutral well-balanced Mahatmas. The sorrows even if few leave an indelible mark and joys, joys are so short-lived that they appear petty in front of sorrows. Only those who are very lucky, whose life—fabric has not been tainted by indelible inks of sorrow would wish for a rebirth. The multitudes are always striving for moksha—freedom from the cycle of birth and rebirth—by holy dips, traversing the snow clad mountains, visiting the shrines and doing all that is prescribed to them by rule books and those who have mastered these books. A desire to escape the miserable present, a wish not to return back to it in future, an urge to cast a veil over it, a hope that the veil is never lifted.

But what was Sulochana thinking lying on her bed staring at the walls around her? Sulochana—the beautiful eyed. Beautiful brown eyes, bright eyes. Time had played mischief only with the eyesight and the area around her eyes. Perhaps her grandfather had not fathomed, as he christened her Sulochana, what the beautiful eyes would be destined to see.

Eyes that brimmed up with tears as memories rushed in to fill the vacuum of loneliness, for nature hates vacuum. Nature hates vacuum, but the phenomenon of vacuum nevertheless exists. It exists in the life of an old woman still breathing, or breathing still on a floor of a tall building in a city of strangers, rather a city that had estranged her. Strangers who exalted the companionship of loneliness amidst circles of friends and loved ones over a hot cup of tea were easy to spot. But those who had been truly washed away to the farthest more shores of human bonds and connections could not be expected to even narrate their tale to anyone.

Oh! The tea had been boiling for a long while now, reduced to almost half a cup. She must hurry up and pour it in her cup. Cup of tea flavoured with dry ginger had been a good companion, a mute one though. But its companionship too was timed-till she was able to make one.

Whole day long the sun measured the distance between the two sides of Sulochna's bed in the verandah-a distance so short and yet so long that it always measured up to a day. The sun, so bright, its warmth breathed life in her, through her skin into her bones each day. Sunlight, they say, conquers darkness. But it fails to pierce through the gloominess of a woman in the twilight of her age. Sulochana got up and looked down from her gallery. She saw women basking in the sun, talking and laughing. While middle aged women knitted, women her age peeled and ate oranges. Nothing could be heard distinctly but they made a lot of noise.

"Come Sulochana. Come downstairs.What do you keep doing all alone up there? Come!" One of them invited Sulochana but she smiled and refused politely. No, she decided she would not join them. Joining them meant talking to them, telling them about her self and what would she tell? There was no common ground for carrying on a conversation with them even over such trifles as the kind of fabric they preferred. Bosky would sound too odd in a land of lizzy-bizzy. She had a great repertoire of tales—of times gone by, of people dead and long forgotten, of political upheavals. But who would care to lend her an ear. And who could say the invitation was genuine. Maybe, it was just a show of courtesy. Did they really want her to join them? Did Sulochana also sense this show off?

She kept standing and looking at the houses neatly lined in front. Only one of them remained obscured as it had a huge mango tree growing in its garden. The owner of the house lay dozing off on a chair as sunshine lulled him to sleep. She wondered how old the man might be, her own age maybe, or maybe a few years older.

"No, I will not wear a burqa! And why should I when I am not a mussalman."

She remembered she had revolted as a young girl only to be coaxed into wearing it by Vasakhi. She had never learnt to say no to him since the night he had lifted the veil of red dupatta that a shy Sulochana had covered her face with—the veil that fuels passions on both its sides.

"Reshmo! The world suddenly looks less bright, less cheerful." She had lamented adjusting herself in the tonga.

"Come on now, don't complain. You know we are already living in troubled times," Reshmo had shouted back.

"But what do the troubles of the world have to do with veiling Sulochana? Is Sulochana so beautiful that her beauty interferes with the troubles of the world," she had protested. "Tongawalla, to Lady Griffith Government Model High School, quick." Reshmo had tried to ignore her complaints, "You question a lot. Am I not right in telling them not to get their women educated? This is what they do when they start going to schools—lick your heads clean."

Sulochana reclined on the chair staring at the dull wall in front, fear clawing at her heart. Fear, fears that she lived with. Fears that she compromised with, fears that stared at her in the face, fears that she fought against, each passing day. No noise, no sound, no clamouring of swords. A silent fight against a silent enemy. Fear of death, of going to unfamiliar places, of not being able to see her loved ones again? Yes her loved ones that still lived; well she had learnt to love them. If only one could learn well enough. But she had learnt to live, if not live well enough.

Whose laughter was it that rent the emptiness of Sulochana's room? Her own perhaps. She could even see herself hopping and skipping and fleeting up and down the stairs of her house at Peshawar while other women churned curd and made preparations for the afternoon meal. "Blue, orange, green, blue . . . . ," she could hear little children counting the coloured pieces of glass fixed in the window.

"Reshmo, you know, Miss Gregory tells us that knowledge lifts the veil over ignorance and that the sun never sets in Great Britain and that the sea further meets the ocean and that the earth that appears flat is actually round."

At this Reshmo had been convinced that the khadi clad young men were right when they said that the English were merely fooling them all.

But the hopping and skipping was soon over. Now it was but a drag left. For how long would the drag continue and where did it lead to? To an end, perhaps. Perhaps, to a deliverance from this emptiness.

Day is finished as soon as the night casts a veil over it. Night, when scary long shadows dance on the walls. Long shadows, which amuse one in childhood turn scarier with age. A child shares his fears with others but the aged learns to live with them. And who to share them with? People come, people leave. But shadows return each night to haunt. The shadows of the summer of 1947, when there had been some violent processions followed by firing and the curfew. Situation was very tense. The leaders had bartered peace for peace of mind. Not one, but two nations were taking birth. The labour pains had started. Labour pains had started but there was no doctor around. The English doctor who was called in even at a sneeze was not available at this critical hour. Sulochana had writhed in pain. But the fortress of power politics has forever been invincible to the cries of a woman, for the business of power must go on undisturbed.

"They have looted us, they have plundered us, they have cheated on us."

She remembered Vasakhi lamenting and sobbing. Vasakhi who had been transformed from one man to several pieces of a man, exiled to a land he had no associations with.

"Where are my people? Where are my bazaars? Where is my land? Who am I? He had cried. "The uprooted flowers of spring do not live to see another spring. Do they Sulochana?" His choking voice still echoed in her ears.

It was summer and the mango tree had blossomed again this year, like every other year gone by, like it always will for years to come. Blossoming year after year after year—nature knows the art of flowering, blooming, fruiting, rejuvenating eternally. But not so for the lives of men. Men—the fruits that must detach themselves from the branch of the tree they grow on. They may even be plucked before ripening. But a ripened fruit must not remain on the branch for long for the result inevitably is rotting. Sulochana watched bunches of the green unripe mangoes sway with the light breeze. She noticed with interest groups of children arrive armed with stones. They hit the mango bunches and quickly hid behind the hedge encircling the house. A bunch fell. Sulochana waited for the old man to run out madly shouting at children and cursing them. Often it was difficult to tell what gave more pleasure to the children—the reward of raw mangoes or the sulking and running after of an irritated old fellow. But the obvious did not happen and the children gladly walked away with their trophy.

Each day after that the children kept pelting stones at the mango tree devoid of any fear of the sulk. It was then that Sulochana realized that the veil had extended over to the old sulk, that it was a veiled existence that people like her lead. Unlike humans, the veil did not distinguish between men and women. It veiled them alike. It kept walling them in, in their existence till they passed into oblivion. It kept enveloping them till they were sealed away from human consciousness. The veil estranged all that was on the other side. Yes, it did suffocate but now there was no resentment.

Along the Banks

Murlidhar launched his boat into the cool waters of the river after applying vermillion to it and saying a little prayer. It was a daily ritual he performed. It was better to start the day with a little prayer than venture into the river with a mind full of doubts. But he trusted the river. The river had never betrayed him. He aptly called it 'Maiyya' for like a mother it took care of all his needs as he earned his living by ferrying people across it.

Drop by drop the snow melts. Frozen for so long but it melts. Melt it must if it has to flow, flow as a river does. River that reaches out, out to waiting millions, the desperate millions. Who ever chalked the course of a river? It decides one for itself amidst the dark scary shadows of giant mountains. The river performs the 'mahayagya' of 'reaching out' accepting all the 'aahutis' of innumerable tiny streams that join in. The river splashes and falls and turns and bends and loops and meanders but never gives up its flow for flow is everything. The one that gets lost in the sands of time nevertheless flows; flowing ceaselessly in the entire consciousness.

The river was flowing, skipping ahead. Its waters, now orangish red, now golden as sunrays took their holy dip as the sun applied vermillion all over the river in reverence. People had already started thronging the ghats to perform puja and pay obeisance. It was always a flattered river that left the ghats and resumed its lonely journey.

"Now haven't they again pampered you? Why, you almost swell and widen by the time you leave the ghats," said the tree icily. The river ignored his remarks. She knew why the tree was always so smitten. Not many pilgrims trekked up to it to tie the sacred thread and make a wish. 'Poor wish-granting huge tree!' was how the river always teased him. "Cheer up tree! Look what! Today Murli's ferrying some youngsters. And I bet they would trek up to you" the tree was alarmed at what the river had just said. He observed the newcomers as they were indeed coming closer.

"Hmmm, an old tree. How old do you think it must be" remarked one.

"Hey look it's a wish-granting tree. Just look at the threads people have tied all over its branches" said another.

"Do you think a tree can grant wishes," others shouted. The tree keenly waited for the answer.

"Well, I wonder and anyway who keeps a track record of the ones that were granted and ones that were not" someone from the group remarked.

"It is all a matter of faith. What do you say Kirti?" the blue shirt looked inquisitively at Kirti.

But Kirti did not say anything. She only looked up with wondrous eyes at the huge canopy of the old tree with several strands of red sacred threads hanging from its branches.

"Hey! Come on, let's make a wish." The blue shirt had hardly finished speaking when they all pulled out the puja—threads from their thalis and each one tied a wish to the branch of the tree, closed their eyes and prayed for the wish to get fulfilled. But Kirti did not tie the sacred thread. For once the tree saw hands reach out to its branches but then she withdrew them and quietly put the thread in the puja—thali.

The tree was disappointed and the river could clearly sense this.

"Don't you think the young girl wants to make a wish?" questioned the river.

"But she did not make one" answered the tree.

"And why?" again asked the river.

"How could I tell" the tree spoke.

"Hmm, I think I understand why" remarked the river.

"Why" the tree questioned.

"She doubts."

"She doubts what?"

"She doubts, well, my dear tree, she doubts your abilities to grant her wish" said a reluctant river.

"So, Murli who always ferried wishes has now started ferrying doubts" said the tree, a little hurt.

The koel perched on its branches sensed the hurt and lent it an echo in her song. The tree was quiet for the rest of the day. The river could not get him to talk no matter how hard she tried.

"Oh, come on tree, cheer up or one swift current and your long bent branches are gone forever." Even her threats could not lift up the spirits of the tree.

Soon it was dark and the ghats were humming with activity. Devotees were positioning themselves for the *Aarti* of the river. Women were covering their heads with the ends of their sarees and arranging the diyas on their thalis. The head priest held a huge lamp lit with numerous wicks all burning bright. Climbing a raised platform he started singing the Aarti and waving the lamp in air as everyone clapped and chorused the Aarti. Kirti kept her eyes closed in deep reverence to the Mother river, opening them only occasionally to feel the brightness of lamps around her, again closing them with deep breaths inhaling the fragrance of incense sticks as ringing of bells deafened her mind to disturbing thoughts.

When they had all left and there was silence all over did the moon alight with its retinue of stars, so that the scalding souls burning day and night could get some cooling relief. The river implored them to get the tree talking. "No holy river, forgive us, for we only influence and never interfere in the matters concerning the earth" was their curt reply.

Morning at the ghats saw Murlidhar ferrying people across. It even saw Tanna, the bard, sit in meditative silence on the steps of the ghat after flexing his muscles. It did not miss seeing Champa and Chameli—those two sisters who sold flowers at the banks of the river—threading flowers to make lavish garlands. Champa did not like Murlidhar nor did Chameli, even though he was a young bachelor with a glowing dark complexion. Each time Murli passed by their stall he stopped for a moment, looked up at the two sisters, gave a charming smile which Champa said was rather wry and Chameli insisted was frivolous. How could they ever like someone who never bought a single flower from their stall and only kept smiling?

"It is not for smiles that we get up early each morning when the world is still dreaming away, to pluck flowers from the garden" lamented Champa.

"Look, how the roses pricked my fingers this morning," Chameli said showing her fingers to her sister.

"Thorns, not roses that pricked," corrected Champa as she carried on with threading the flowers to make garlands. And when she had finished she took the garland in her hands and admiring her piece of art declared, "Don't you think this one is fit enough to find a place right over the crown of the Gods." Murlidhar heard it just as he was passing by. He even stood for a moment to accompany Champa in admiring her art. But when Chameli got ready to pounce at him like an infuriated cat he gave his disarming smile freezing the sisters in their frames and left.

The river leapt up to see the spectacle and laughed and her laughter murmured in the deep valleys. Her infectious laughter touched the tree and its branches began swaying from side to side.

"But I must say they disappoint me when they doubt me— I who pumps oxygen into the lungs of this world". The tree broke the long spell of silence.

"But doubting only shows how desperate they are at believing – one final plugging of all loopholes before they plunge to faith," argued the river.

"You women! You are all too difficult," retorted the tree.

Now the river was furious and the men at the waterworks reported a slight rise in the water levels as they kept a constant vigil on the scale.

"Don't you call me a woman, don't you know

I overflow my banks – they do not.

I revolt and storm into men's fortresses – they do not.

I make my fury inescapable – they can not.

I weather down elevations and fill depressions – they can not.

I am the great Equalizer – they are still sorting out their equality."

The tree was left speechless and its branches drooped down as if kneeling in front of the infuriated mighty river. The river water gushed and rushed and inadvertently splashed on Murli's face.

"Oh Maiyya, calm down, calm down Maiyya," he pleaded and only then did the river regain her serenity.

Champa stood on the ghat looking in the direction the river went. This was something she liked observing on hot afternoons when they were not many people at the ghat. This was also the activity that Tanna indulged in – plain gazing at the river searching for something only he knew what. The river seemed to Champa to stretch from one infinity to another.

Ostensibly without a beginning, without an end, the river flowed on. The sight of swirling waters flowing on plucked a few strings of Champa's heart and played a melancholic note. The tiny pearl like tears must have weighed a ton for she always felt lighter and better after she had shed a few. What made her sad, she could never know. Perhaps it was the loneliness of the journey of the river and of life itself that stretched from one unknown into the other lesser known. Companionship, if any, was always bound within the limits of time and space. Staring for so long made her almost fall with dizziness in the direction the river flowed. Had it not been for the timely intervention of a firm grip that pulled her back, she had almost lost her balance and fallen in to the river.

On regaining her balance, Champa was only too agitated to find that it was none other than Murlidhar who was now pealing with laughter. "Ah, you!" Champa gave one angry glance and started to go without thanking Murli. She turned once more to look at him but to her dismay found him toying with her clip. She ran her fingers through her hair to ascertain if it was the same clip.

Yes it was indeed it. The one that had a peacock carved on it. The one she had bought at the fair. She could leave it and go her way, she thought. But what mischief might just brew up in Murli's head? Who could tell?

"Give me back my clip!"

"On one condition."

"What condition?"

"Allow me to place it back in your hair!"

Champa looked around. There were not many people at the ghat at that time of the day. Tanna was anyway too absorbed in gazing at the flowing waters. Before Champa could nod, Murli sprang up to her and started gathering her ruffled hair. Champa could sense that there was something really relaxing, rather magical, about his hands that stroked her hair. She closed her eyes and stood for what seemed like an age; so peaceful, so rejuvenated. She became conscious of her being only when Murli had done his job and whispered in her ear, "Wake up, my dear." She gave Murli a look more annoyed than ever before and resumed her way home.

In the evening when the sisters went to the temple they were delighted to see the crown of the Gods adorned with the garland that Champa had so lovingly made.

The wishes had been hanging from the branches of the tree for a long time. They had most grudgingly borne the scorching heat of summers. Now they were tired of hanging for so long waiting for the monsoon winds. Had it not been for the shade of the tree and coolness of the river they would have suffocated to nothingness. The wishes vied with each other for some space of their own. They looked at every new entrant with suspicion for the ones that asked for might were tied next to those asking for right, the ones for prosperity were next to those for contentment, the ones that sought bonding were tied next to those desiring moksha. But the most scandalous pair that put even the tree in a dilemma was the one that asked for successful completion of a dam across the river and the one that aimed at preserving the river valley in its nascent form.

The wishes swayed in the direction the wind blew. Which ones were ultimately fulfilled all depended on how favourable the direction of the wind was for them. The unlucky ones that had not been fastened with a sure hand often fell into the swirling river.

The sky was overcast. Hordes of thick dark clouds were marching across the sky, threatening the sky which maintained its eloquent silence. The clouds roared. Then perhaps some infighting broke out among their ranks and they clashed their swords waking up lightning from her deep slumber. She glided across the sky and was still gliding when she noticed the wish tree. The storm blew her raven tresses, trying to drag her in the direction the clouds were heading. She resisted the drag and ceased awhile. Poor tree, bachelor tree, so inexperienced at handling earthly beauties and here was a cosmic one lounging at him. He quivered realizing how fatal an attraction such flashing beauty could be. He cowered to give protection to wishes that sought refuge in him. "May I set foot on one of your branches and make a wish, O lovely tree?" The tree stood wide eyed, on the verge of being uprooted, unable to accede to the cosmic wish, unable to concede to it. The lightening laughed and her laughter thundered across the sky. Agape, the tree stared at the stunning beauty, her beaming face, her eyes shutting with intoxication, asking him for a favour he could grant only at his own peril and that of all the other wishes. Waiting with baited breath the tree wondered how long a fraction of a second could get. Just then the whimsical lightning allowed herself to be dragged further so that she may accompany the darkest of clouds. The wishes sighed with relief, realizing how important it was to protect themselves till they finally were fulfilled.

It had rained incessantly and now the river was in spate. The clever sisters had wound up their business to return in more favourable weather. It was no longer feasible for Tanna to search the river for answers during the monsoons so he left with a promise to return during times of greater plausibility.

"I am anguished, I am anguished!" shouted the river.

"I can see that but why?" asked the tree.

"I am anguished at seeing someone return from my banks without quenching his thirst."

"You mean to say that Tanna was thirsty?"

"Why, of course he was. Look at me, look at my enormous expanse and would you believe me if I told you that it lacks that one drop, one tiny little drop that is sufficient to quench a thirst that is as old as time, nay older than time for time is dated."

"But how could a thirst sustain for so long. It would kill."

"Yes how could it sustain. But it has been and will be. It survives in the hope of being quenched finally one fine day. You know what Tanna kept observing sitting on the stairs of the ghat?"

"What?"

"He kept observing in my expanse a vast desert with no trace of water. He kept smacking his dry lips for some respite."

"For how long do you think this could go on; for some day death would conquer Tanna."

"Yes it would conquer Tanna. And then only the thirst would remain. That longing for a drop in the desert would remain. That one drop, that magical drop that will at once quench the thirst of millions gone by, of millions to come. You can take life out of a thirsty man. Can you ever take his thirst away?

"But take my word for it," the tree asserted, "if there is any kind of thirst in this whole world it will always be quenched at the banks of a river."

The river was overwhelmed.

Murlidhar was still ferrying the needy ones even when other boatmen refused to launch their boats in rough river water.

"Ever seen a fool like Murlidhar?" the river roared with laughter.

"No never. He is just one of his kind," the tree answered.

That Pink Thing

Darbari Lal was crouching on the floor. They had spread the durries all around but Darbari wished it were chairs. At his age sitting on the floor was difficult-soon his feet would go numb and then the legs and then changing positions every now and then did not give a dignified look, especially at solemn occasions as these. He waited for the others to arrive, eking out his neck and staring hard from behind his thick glasses.

"Bebe, now how long are you going to take to dress up for the occasion? Now is that long you take to go to a kirya ceremony?" shouted Laadi at her mother-in-law, her voice almost getting hoarse from shouting since early morning. Bebe did not make a reply. She knew what dressing up meant for an old woman like her. Of course there were no curves left to adjust her attire about. She searched for her slippers that had been shoved too far under the charpoy. It was with great effort that she retrieved them. Then adjusting her white dupatta over her head she started to leave with Laadi's voice still following her, "Tell the other women that I was too ill to come and in case they enquire about the illness, I think I can trust you to name a few."

Darbari could see some women huddled in a corner of the room, their heads draped in white dupattas. Today even he had made it a point to arrive in spotless white attire. He could not have arrived otherwise at the kirya ceremony of Pritam who had died a few days ago. Darbari's dhoti was white, his kurta was white and so was his Gandhi topi that he purchased each year from the Khadi Bhandar. His topi gave him a look quite distinct from that of other men around who preferred a headgear tied around the head like a turban. After all, not all had been as enthusiastic about the freedom struggle as had been Darbari when young. Everyone in the village knew that Darbari's Gandhi topi was a mark of respect to the Mahatma he could never meet. Strange are the ways in which a Mahatma and his philosophy touch the way of life of mortals.

Darbari noticed that he was too early at the gathering. Pritam's family members were still doing the running around, making arrangements for the puja. He had exchanged greetings with them when they had passed him by the first time but now as they passed every now and then, Darbari kept his head low, feeling quite uneasy for having been so early. But he had nothing else to do at home. He knew that although time was running out as it did for Pritam, at his age it was time and time alone that he could squander. In fact it was the prospect of chatting with so many others his age that had made him rush early even to such a solemn ceremony. Once in a while he would look around to see if any of his acquaintance had arrived and all that he could see were people he only recognized but did not know. All looked so similar in white. Whether or not the colour imparted any peace of mind to the grieving family, it definitely marked the air with a sadness that touched all those around.

Colours—dull, monotonous ones for grief and brighter ones for happier occasions and moods. Exactly when during the course of evolution man began assigning meanings to colours is hard to tell but that his colour—code keeps passing on in tact from generation to generation is easy to perceive. In fact now the events are made identifiable by the colours they are draped in. White, pure, peaceful, nascent ones for an occasion when colours are banished. But white was not the colour that was presently bothering Darbari. Rather it was pink.

Bebe Ramditti walked but she walked slowly. She knew she had a long distance to travel before she reached Pritam's house—a stretch of some measure through the fields.

"If only I could go back to the comfort of my charpoy. But what would I tell the other women? What excuse would I make for myself? No one bothers if an old woman does or does not attend a joyous occasion but everyone frowns when she fails to turn up at such unhappy ones." These thoughts directed Bebe to her destination. Half way through she sat down on a mound beside the track and looked at the stretch yet not travelled. It was undulating and she had no one to provide her company. From the guardianship of her father to that of her brothers to that of her husband and now finally to that of her sons-that was a long list indeed. But that was it—just a list. She had traversed most of her life—path all alone, never sitting for too long at any goalpost. "For how long will I sit here? In any case I have to travel whatever is left of it," and she resumed her journey.

To his great delight, Darbari noticed his peers Hawela, Dwarka and Sunder all walking up to him. He made an attempt to get up but realized that his numb feet would not allow him. They all squatted around him over the durries. The men were silent for a while.

"I heard the end came towards morning," Dwarka spoke at length.

"Sometime back when I met him, he appeared to be in good health," said Hawela opening his eyes wide with disbelief.

"Hmm, but it has to come some day. Certain as the day break. Only the exact time and place is not known," said Sunder shaking his head.

"Break of day or the end of it?" objected Dwarka. Sunder and Hawela nodded in approval.

"Day—break," muttered Darbari, trying hard not to remember the break of that day.

"Did you say something Darbari?" questioned Dwarka.

"Ah no, nothing," replied Darbari.

"He had even lost his power of speech, few days before the end came," said Hawela. "It happens when the going is slow. The end announces that it is just around the corner. Just listen to the pujariji when he lectures after the puja. The Yama comes, tightens his noose around the neck and then drawing the soul out drags it to the other world while the dying chokes with the last breath," he carried on.

Darbari felt a lump in his throat. This piece of 'knowledge' was something that always suffocated him.

"I hear there wasn't a single piece of new cloth to dress him up when dead. You know they had to summon the darzi at the last minute. Imagine what a disgrace it would have been had they carried him to the pyre in much used clothes," narrated Dwarka in hushed tones.

'New clothes? Yes, one must be wrapped in new clothes when one finally quits', thought Darbari. Why, even his own trunk did not contain anything that fitted the definition of 'new clothes.' It had never occurred to him before. How silly he had been, he thought, to have never gone shopping for the end of his life's journey. Clothes – new clothes to be wrapped up and stored in his trunk. Even as the others carried on chatting, Darbari could not help thinking about clothes. Yes, that was also a piece of cloth, pink in colour, that suddenly flashed across Darbari's mind before he pulled the emergency brakes at his train of thoughts as Sunder's voice came piercing in his ears.

"And by the way, how old do you think he was?" he asked.

"About two years my elder and Darbari, umm let me count . . . . wasn't he four years younger to you?" asked Dwarka.

"No not four, three," replied Darbari squeakily.

'Elder! So I was the elder. When younger are leaving, how long would it take for the elders to reach the exit door', pondered Darbari. Attending such functions had always been a compulsion for him. He had never quite liked attending them. In fact he dreaded them, for it was at such occasions that all those fears that the aged lived with, surfaced, and in their surfacing kept drowning him.

"One takes great pains in raising one's family— wife, children, grandchildren—and then one fine day he himself abandons everyone and leaves for destinations unknown," philosophized Sunder.

Tears welled up in Darbari's eyes. He was reminded of his wife who had left him some years ago. He was also reminded of his two sons and daughters-in-law and five grandchildren. Would he also have to abandon his loved ones just like his wife did, just like Pritam had done, just like everyone has to one fine day? Oh! Why was he here, listening to all this? This that made the going away harder, he thought.

Soon the puja began and the pundit began reciting the mantras. The entire gathering clasped its hands in prayer and closed its eyes to pay homage to the departed soul. Darbari, too, shut his eyes. Instantly the faces of his loved ones made a flashbulb appearance on the empty screen of his mind. His house, then his courtyard and then the incident of that morning when he had gone to remove his white dhoti from the wash line. There! Spread right across his dhoti was the pink bra. He had stood in disbelief, for a while almost petrified. His slender, wrinkled hands had instantly searched for an object to remove the forbidden thing as it lay dangling over his dhoti. "These daughters-in-law! Ugh! How utterly shameless!" He had raged. Looking over his shoulder, to make sure no one was watching, he had found a stick to aid him in extricating his dhoti from the pinky lacy affair. Darbari Lal opened his eyes at once. There was white all around. The Pundit could be heard extolling the virtues of letting the mind meditate over the one thing of prime most importance in the whole world; that to which all must return some day.

After the puja was over, they began to serve the tea.

"And did I tell you what my great grand granny had experienced? The moment they were lighting her pyre, she sat up straight. She said she had returned from the Yamlok! And if we are to go by her version then first there is all darkness, then light, then . . . ," Dwarka did not complete his sentence.

"Then what?" the others chorused.

"Then the cups!" he shouted.

"The cups?" they chorused again.

"I mean to say our tea has arrived," and he smiled.

The others turned around and saw that they were being offered tea and snacks. Darbari noticed the cups as they were placed next to each other on the tray. He knew he was not going to relish his tea today.

The gathering began to dissipate. Ramditti was reminded of the solitary path she would have to tread again, since she had been unable to find any acquaintance that lived in her neighborhood.

She trudged on, wiping sweat from her tanned face. The green fields stretched as far as the eye could see. After every few steps she would halt and straighten her stooping back to be able to look afar and gauge the distance that she was to travel. She was still looking ahead when she noticed that she was not alone on the track. Someone else was also trekking the same path behind her. She wondered for how long she had been followed. Could it be Pritam's ghost? She dare not look back. Equally, she could not contain herself from not looking back. So she turned.

"Ah! Is that you Darbari?"

"Yes Ramditti. You walk so slow and pause very often to catch your breath. Returning from Pritam's? I didn't notice you there," he said.

"But I saw you," she replied.

"How's everyone in the family?" he asked.

"Fine. And in yours?" she asked.

"Good good. God's grace! And how is the pain in your joints?"

"How do you expect it to be at this age? God doesn't get kinder with age. Does he?" she replied.

The old woman and the old man kept talking and walking together.

"The end, the exit, it's difficult. It chokes my throat even as I think of it," spoke Darbari.

"Hmm Darbari, I think it is not as difficult as the journey itself. The end is certain but what one might confront during the journey is uncertain." Ramditti looked thoughtfully at Darbari, and then carried on, "Ah, your house is at the other end then what business makes you head towards mine?"

"I heard there is a fine darzi come to set up his shop somewhere around. Can you tell me where I could find him?" he asked.

"You wouldn't have to look very hard to find him. He has a huge flashy pink hoarding hung outside his shop."

Ramditti's reply sealed Darbari's lips for the rest of the journey.

Henna

As always, Morni was up early morning and was dusting the whole house. She dusted the furniture, the bookrack, the toy rack, the doors, the windows, the curtains, why, she even dusted the walls; if only she could reach up to the ceiling. Oh why had the entire world's dust settled in her house? She could not comprehend. But it was the dusting and not the dust that had already started getting on Amrita's nerves as also on younger Nikki's nerves.

"Pause for a moment Ma and at least tell me where my bag is. I am already late for work," crooned Amrita.

"There on that chair and listen don't just get stuck on to your chair. Try to make it home early, for these winter days it gets dark quite early," shouted Morni.

"And where are my books Mama, I have my exams approaching," asked young Nikki.

"There on the rack and don't you bother me now." Giving a stern look Morni resumed her attempts at making her world spick and span. Nikki was anyway used to getting such stern looks and terse replies. She understood too well that not many grown ups felt that the young ones ought to be treated with some measure of deference—sensitive age, moulding personalities, ego development and all that stuff. After all she had been attending school, the temple of learning, of training young impressionable minds, place where self-esteem begins to take shape. Only yesterday she had been made to stand on the stage in the assembly hall where the teachers pointed out to the students that that was neither the shape nor the shade of the sweater that they were supposed to wear to school and that was also not the way their socks ought to droop down. How Nikki had yearned to climb the school stage and how much she now despised it. If only they had given her a chance to argue. Perhaps she could have then convinced them that it is gravity that pulls down the socks.

It was not before noon that the house was scrupulously clean as was also Morni after a thorough bath. But being clean was not the same as being pure and who better understood this than did Morni. She boiled a concoction to sprinkle over the entire place, every nook, each corner. Alas! The house was livable once more. Tomorrow again it would not be before noon that the house would become tidy enough to house Morni and her two daughters.

Life for Morni moved one day at a time. But in this whole day it was the evenings she yearned for. Evenings—when she would stand at the gate waiting most eagerly for a wandering seller of scrubbers, vipers, brooms, dusters and the like. Her efforts at keeping her world clean left her with worn out brooms and dusters and vipers too often—hence her passion for the wandering seller's wares. But wasn't it the first and the most important Rule of the Fraternity of Widows to keep their world as clean as clean could be? To express her solidarity for the cause of the fraternity she even clad herself in spotless white attire. And as a corollary to the Rule she kept her passions burning for the wanderer and his wares.

"What do you keep reading nose down in your books Nikki?" Morni asked affectionately looking up as she continued grinding spices. Nikki who was only waiting to be distracted from the boredom of books, pointed at the title page.

"History!"

"And what all do you read in that?"

"It's the story of men. Men who went to war, made peace, breached peace, again went to war, then in between invented something and discovered some other things."

"All about men? A sinister book to be read at your age." Nikki giggled as Morni continued, "Men achieved so much outside the house and look how women like me remained ignorant of much of it. Perhaps it's because men returned home as mere men—hungry for food, weary for sleep, in need of getting their soiled clothes washed." Morni spoke thoughtfully then carried on with grinding spices with pestle and mortar.

"Oh Mama, you think so much. And I thought it was only cleanliness that kept your mind occupied." Morni looked up and smiled at her daughter's remarks.

"You keep the house so clean mama but I don't understand why you never clean up the dirty spots at the front wall just next to the main door?"

"Which ones Nikki?"

"The brown ones at the entrance."

"Silly girl! They are not any dirty spots but imprints of my henna adorned hands when I first entered this house as a young bride. Spots is what remains." Tears welled up in Morni's eyes by the time she finished her sentence and Nikki, realizing the sensitivity of the issue, resumed her lessons in history.

Mother and daughter were soon startled when the door bell rang. Strange how such unimportant things startle some people. Morni looked up at the clock. It was not time yet for Amrita to return. Then who could it be? Relatives or maybe friends? No, no; they had not rung her bell all these five years that her husband left, why would they now? With a mind full of doubts Morni opened the door. It was the postman who held out a registered card to her. She called out to Nikki who signed and received it.

"Oh Mama! It's a wedding invitation." She exclaimed.

"Read and tell me all about it quick!" the excitement in Morni's voice was too pronounced.

"It's aunt Vijaya's younger daughter's wedding. Vijaya? Isn't she papa's elder sister?"

"Yes of course. I always knew Vijaya was not like the rest. I knew she would never forget us during celebration time."

"But Mama how can we go? The wedding's just a few days before my exams."

"Oh come on. Study hard now. It's once in a while such an occasion arrives. Imagine how much you'd enjoy. Just imagine we'll get to meet all our relatives after so long."

Morni couldn't wait for the hour when Amrita would knock at the door. Amrita had not even knocked when Morni opened the door and began telling her all about the invitation.

"Oh Mama, come on. Can't you see it's less of an invitation and more of a newsletter to let us know that happiness still knocks at their door?"

"Amrita Amrita! Now that you have started earning that doesn't mean you'll decide what I have to do and what not."

"Now when did I say anything of that sort?"

"We are leaving tomorrow and that's final! Besides it's an hour's journey anyway."

Having locked her doors Morni stepped on to the street, her daughters following at close heels with suitcases and bags. There was someone who passed by. Someone who yearned for Morni to merely cast her glance at his wares. The wares that gave some meaning to the otherwise mundane existence of Morni. It had taken so long to nurture the bond that Morni shared with the vendor's wares. How could she snap it all of a sudden? The wares were indeed clueless. They questioned but Morni was in no mood to answer. Tossing her hair back she walked upright on the street, her ears already ringing with the animated tones of all those who had cared to remember her in their hour of jubilation. The vendor felt cheated. It was more than he and his wares could bear. Both decided not to tread the lane that led to heartless Morni's house ever again.

Constant chattering and laughter of women could be heard above the playing of loud music. Morni's heart had begun thumping hard right at the gate. It skipped a beat when she entered through the door and stood in the hall jam-packed with women. It was the Mehndi ki Raat. There in a corner young girls were flocking the mehndiwallah. Nikki dropped the bags and rushed to the corner. Amrita followed suit. At the centre sat the women playing the dholak, while some other women kept pleading them to save their energies till the photographer had arrived. But the joy and enthusiasm of women knew no bounds. It had been five long years but Morni reckoned the faces of those who sang and danced. More than time it is the circumstances that bring about a change in the countenance of people. Looking at their faces it became obvious that nothing unusual had happened in their lives.

Mehandiwallah was portraying intricate patterns over the outstretched palms. He was finding it hard to please the fussy girls. While some demanded Arabic patterns, there were others who insisted on more traditional ones with peacocks and floral motifs. While some wanted finer strokes others desired thicker, broader strokes.

Morni listened intently to the songs. The melodies had changed. The beats had become faster. But the lyrics were the same. Same as they had been at her marriage. Lyrics that complained of the ruthless ritual of married daughters leaving their parental home, lyrics that wished prosperity and fertility for the young bride, lyrics that teased and mocked at the in-laws. There, standing near the door, Morni could see Vijaya wiping her eyes with the ends of her dupatta for they were the songs that brought tears to Vijaya's eyes. They were also the songs that brought tears to Morni's eyes. A thin film of tears still occluding her sight, Morni nodded at Vijaya. She nodded at some other women as well. Nodding? Was that all? Morni wondered standing at the door. No warm welcome? No affectionate hugs? Did no one have to ask her how she had survived these five years? No, they did not have anything to ask a widow with the liability of two young, unmarried daughters. But she had. But no law allows the accused to ask questions standing in the witness box.

Morni looked here and there. If only someone would call out her name. She was amidst her relatives, her own people. If Vijayaa was busy accepting greetings, then there were Usha, Nita, Asha and so many more faces she reckoned. Women nudged each other as she passed by for she could see elbows that rose. Women whispered in each others ears as she passed by for their whispers were meant for her ears.

"Look, listen, I am Morni, the same person you always knew. It is only my dupatta that wears a dull drab look", pleaded Morni's bent head. Accused, she stood ashamed in the witness-box. The crime—what right does a penniless widow with the liability of two unmarried daughters have to be in the company of those who had disposed of their liabilities. The judgement—no the judge did not pronounce the judgement; he only whispered it to others, who whispered it to still others, who nudged others— leaving the criminal in the witness box forever.

Amrita and Nikki were drying the henna applied over their palms when they noticed their mother approaching. "Look Ma, isn't this beautiful!" the girls chorused. Morni caught her dupatta by its ends and started wiping Amrita's hands as also Nikki's hands.

"Wait Ma! Just what are you doing?" shouted Amrita.

"Please Ma, look it has not even dried," cried Nikki. But an unrepentant Morni kept wiping every trace of mehndi off her daughters' palms.

Nobody noticed when a widow and her two daughters left, boarding the last bus that was plying that night.

Morni was too relieved to be back home. It made little difference to Amrita. Only Nikki was cross. Morni bolted her door and fastened it well and then again checked if the bolt was in its place before she went to sleep.

The night was dark, very dark. But in this darkness there were three women plucking leaves from a thorny bush. Morni tried to recognize them but how could she tell when the women kept their faces veiled. Morni asked them what business they had plucking leaves in the middle of the night. But they did not reply. They plucked and dropped the leaves in a basket kept on the ground. Morni gathered some courage, went closer and looked into the basket. But the basket was empty. No matter how many leaves they plucked, the basket remained empty. Now blood had started dripping from the hands of one of them. It was the thorns, the thorns from the bush, long spikes, several of them embedded in her palms. It was the spiky bush of henna. Morni gave out a loud cry and woke up horrified.

"Ma, Ma wake up! Look it's me. What happened?"

Morni clutched her daughter by the arm, held her tight and then looked hard at her palms.

"Why, what happened?" asked Amrita. Morni did not answer but her face clearly wore a look of relief. She longed for the day to dawn and dawn soon, for the urge to dust her house and set her eyes once again on the wandering vendor's wares was getting too unbearable for her.

Garden

The doors were shut. Thick heavy curtains were drawn against the windows. The only source of fresh air was perhaps the wire – gauze of the kitchen window. He was all alone inside. No sound, no noise—a silent existence in a closed house. So quiet was the house that any passerby would have assumed that the dwellers were off on a vacation.

The patch of green at the front had not been mowed for several months now, while in the backyard wilderness ran amuck. Tall Ashoka trees marked the boundary of this wilderness as if trying to delineate this madness from whatever sanity stretched on the other side. Whosoever had planted them must have had on mind the peculiar property of the trees to absorb sound. Whatever was heard on either side was not conveyed to the other. The wild garden thrived unperturbed by the sounds of sense outside.

The stout mango tree stood somberly, the henchman of the garden, extending his thickly muscled arms over the sides. The prickly lemon tree pierced shot its branches in all directions possible. So what if it was short in stature? It had not forsaken its right to horizontal development. Its slender branches kept shooting around.

Bunches of luscious litchis kept drooping from the litchi tree. Pears had lagged in this ripening season and the pear did not afford a fully laden look as that of the litchi. Nevertheless the two trees had acquired a high status—the one that accompanies prosperity. The guava tree stood impoverished in sharp contrast to its neighbours. The chikoo tree could be least bothered and anyway it was still a fledgling. Towering above the rest stood the giants of the garden. What species they belonged to? No one dare ask the Giants such nasty questions. When could the dwarfs bother the giants? Nevertheless the giants were the cause of perpetual botheration to the grass growing down below. They kept shedding their deep brown spiky dry leaves over the succulent lush green strands of grass. Now no one likes their hairstyle being spoilt every now and then; also when the hairstyling had been long overdue and patches of baldness had begun to appear.

A crow sat cawing on a branch of the guava. "Oh shit!" cried the tree.

"Did you say something?" the crow was taken aback by this sudden interruption to his monotonous cawing.

"There's no use arguing with you liberated souls but you must never forget that your freedom ends where my hygiene begins," cried the tree.

Whole day the sun kept blazing, its rays knocking hard at the door trying their level best to awaken the slumbering soul but the knocks fell on deaf ears. The sun traveled and traveled right across the sky to reach the front door of the house. The rays knocked with glaring ferocity but the occupant of the house was in no mood to let even a single ray to trickle into his gloom that had been well air-conditioned. At last the sun was tired, its energy pent up. It decided to settle down behind the mountains and retire for the night.

Dry leaves lay piled up in a corner. Not that they liked being there, ostracized in that spot. But then the wind had shoved them there and now they lay in heaps— brown, black, torn, shorn, rotting leaves. They would have preferred being scattered all over the place but then it is not in the ambit of the downtrodden to decide what treatment befits them. Rather it is under the jurisdiction of those higher-ups in the power hierarchy. The dry ones envied those green ones fixed firmly on the branches.

The wind started blowing with ferocious velocity. She lashed mercilessly against all that stood obstructing her path. Whole day it had been simmering hot and now it was the fury of the wind that was becoming unbearable. No, the wind did not appreciate her path being lit and so snapped the electric paraphernalia, switching off bulbs whichever way she went. "Huh! The mortals thought they could dot my path with the cosmetics of their technology. Don't I know where I am heading to?"

The wind was rushing past. Then it stopped all of a sudden. She sat for a while over the high fence of the garden. 'No there is no point in moving so fast,' it occurred to her almost in a flash. Perhaps she should rest for a while before proceeding on the arduous journey, she thought.

Dry leaves could have some respite. But they were upset anyhow.

"She has no business tossing us up in mid-air, shredding us and banging us against the walls against our will. Mercy Lord! Must we crash land hither thither?"

"Now what?" grumbled a leaf as it lay flat on the ground.

"Who knows what goes on in her mind?" whined the one lying next.

"Ever seen a woman with such high B.P.?" intervened a fallen twig.

"B.P.? No you mean H.P.?" said an uprooted flower nursing it's bruised petals.

The trees stood motionless, maintaining their defensive postures fearing the worst that could happen on such a night.

Next day when the crow sat cawing at a branch of the guava tree, the tree took the opportunity to ask what had been bugging it since the last night.

"Where do you think she keeps rushing to on such lonely nights?"

The crow adjusted himself on the branch, gave a pause as if lost in deep contemplation, then crooned at length.

"You know where the far-far land is?"

"No I don't. It's not in the nature of things stationary to know of far off places."

"Well, well, ignorant as you are," now the guava could feel the heat of the air of contempt surrounding the crow as he carried on, "there in that far of land," the guava interrupted him before he could finish speaking.

"Ignorant as I am but not naïve enough to believe that crows can fly to such far of lands."

"Now when did I say I visited the place personally?" the crow was now trapped. "It is as I gather from my communication web."

"Now is there anything about the far off lands that you wish to tell me or is that all?" the guava was irked.

"There in that far off land lives her lover Mr. Thunderstorm, lying asleep under the magic spell of a Wicca. With her fury, as you witnessed last night, the wind raises him out of his slumber, breaking his dormancy. Then what follows their meeting is havoc."

The guava tree stood agape. The litchi tree had been overhearing their conversation and now the litchis began to blush. The pear tree shook its head in amazement and in the process dropped a few unripe fruits. The lemon was bitter; how could anyone love someone with such force he could not fathom. How could he when no one, neither the crow nor the koel, had ever extended a hand of friendship at him. Ah! The short always have a grudge, a prick somewhere. Meanwhile the giants shed a few leaves, affronting the grass below and the Ashoka absorbed all the sounds lest the secret be communicated to the world outside.

"Do you think I am going to believe the stories that you cook up," blurted the guava at length.

"You don't? Go ahead ask the Chinese palm and you'll know the truth." The crow was upset.

"Hey you! You Chinese palm! Is the crow cawing the truth?" guava enquired.

But the addressee here was in no mood to reply to those who called it names.

'Chinese palm Chinese palm,' they were no Chinese palm tree. Just a bunch of Japanese fans tied neatly together and stacked in a corner by the vendor who had gone on an errand and would be back anytime.

The fans kept silent, paying no attention to the crass creatures around, their tasseled ends swaying delicately with the flowing air.

It was a hot afternoon and the koel was busy singing a melody to the henchman. The melody was enchanting but it kept interfering with the siesta of guava.

"God knows what goes on between the koel and the mango tree," said guava.

"Ah! Even I don't know," the crow spoke drowsily.

"Thank god there is something that you don't know!" guava was jolted out of his sluggishness.

"Hah! No one can. She hides too much. You hardly get to see her," cried the crow. "But I have a hunch."

"What?" queried the guava.

"I think she is a smart marketing agent cum businesswoman who has coaxed the mango tree into believing that it is her singing that is going to ripen and sweeten his mangoes every season."

"Is that so?" the guava was surprised at the revelation. "I think there is an element of truth in your words this time. Even I have noticed this relation between her singing and his ripening and sweetening. But isn't that strange. Even I eavesdrop on her songs but her singing has nothing to do with my ripening and sweetening."

"And worming," muttered the crow as the taste of the guavas he had eaten the last time lingered in his mouth. Ugh! How over-ripe and full of vermin.

"Did you say something," the guava asked still pondering over the issue.

"Ah no, nothing really, and where were we," he carried on, "yes as I said earlier it is a pact between the two—all the sweetness of her voice gets carried on in to his mangoes and he in turn shelters and shields her. And you expected eavesdropping to achieve for you what the mango achieves with close embraces!"

Aided by the company of his friend, the crow mapped the entire garden. Crows must keep themselves abreast of all that goes on around or who would go and inform a housewife lounging leisurely that guests are expected anytime—much earlier than the telephone ring and even in case the guest prefers arriving without telling. One of the Ashokas was leaning against the one adjacent to it and this new development did not escape the crow's keen sight.

" Hey Gavy dear, look! There, that slender Ashoka is almost falling over the other."

"Oh them! They are bosom friends. Must be whispering something in the other's ear. Right since the day the wind started blowing, these maidens in green tunics are practicing dance steps. Just wait for the wind to blow and watch!"

As the wind blew, the crow watched the girls bending and straightening synchronously.

"Crazy ha!" the crow immensely enjoyed what he saw.

It had drizzled that morning; a pre-monsoon shower, a reminder that the monsoon was on its way. The dust in the air had been sprinkled over the leaves and the otherwise spotless green leaves now gave the appearance of a floor most unwillingly mopped. The guava was sulking since morning but the crow, while giving a patient listening to his friend, was busy admiring the chameleon.

"Marvellous!"

"I don't understand what could be marvelous on such a day?"

"The chameleon! Just look the way he is balancing himself on the trunk of that tree raising his torso."

"Oh him! He performs yogasans everyday and this one's called the bhujangasana. It keeps his back strong and flexible."

The sight was tickling his palettes when the guava diverted his attention.

"Hey before I forget, you are invited tonight."

"And where?"

"My dear crow, at the annual ritual of the frogs."

"Ah, that summer madness. I guess when the temperatures soar and pre monsoon showers arrive, their souls get possessed."

"Ya, and they collect by the scores carrying out a procession through the night."

"I would rather call it the Mahapanchayat— a grand assembly of the froggies. But it is a late night show and I am too drowsy by sundown. However you'll be there Gavy, wouldn't you?"

"I have no other choice."

The crow was up early the next morning and the guava was also eagerly waiting for him to give him a word for word account of the past night.

"The stage was set. There was perfect silence. Then the guests hopped and leapt in. The moon rose higher to light up the whole area. I wonder why they keep taking such heavenly favours when that electric pole out there was already illumining the spot free of cost." Hearing this, the giants sighed and shed a few leaves. "And you know what, that Raat ki Rani, the one growing a few feet from here, she had worn such a lot of perfume. I guess she empties entire vials. She had flooded the entire garden with her fragrance last night."

"But I can't sniff a trace right now."

"Don't you know she casts off her scented gowns by the morning and sends them to the laundryman? Never wears the same attire the next morning. She is a rani after all. Yes, and she stood so close I was almost on the verge of fainting."

"Fainting or swooning?"

"Whatever you may prefer."

"But what about the grand assembly?"

"How could I know when they all kept leaping and croaking and jumping and tripping the whole night?"

The monsoon came rumbling and thundering and it poured for days on end. It gave a thorough washing to the entire garden. Nature revealed its true colours— verdant, sparkling, radiant— its true odours— fresh, refreshing. The crow got wet each time he came over to meet his pal. His neatly combed feathers got ruffled to give him a very shoddy look. The guava too did not have much to talk about as he stood facing the fury of the moisture laden winds. The squirrels kept their fur spick and span by navigating over the highways and flyovers of intertwining branches of trees. The inhabitant of the house kept the flavours of the season at bay by extending the sheet of tarpaulin over the windows and doors.

One wintry afternoon as the crow lay perched on the guava, basking in the warm sunshine, the guava gave a sudden cry of horror as his peace was disturbed by a cracking sound.

"Look, behold Crow! The door opens at last."

"Ha it creaks. And who are those creatures? Men men! But why are they wielding axes?"

"Must be out to gather some dead wood. Why even some of my branches need trimming and sculpting, don't they?"

"Yeah they are approaching us."

"Let them come. I am ready for the makeover."

The shining blades struck at the main trunk of the guava as it gave out loud painful cries. But the only thing that the hard of hearing could hear was the chipping of wood. The crow was too appalled to think of a way to react but guided by his instincts he began to peck at the men. But shooing him away was no big deal for the men. The axes struck at the maidens in green tunics, they ripped apart the Japanese fans, pulled down the blushing litchi, did not spare the juvenile chikoo that anyway fell at a single blow. The muscled henchman gave a tough fight before he lay motionless bearing the melody of the koel's song in his heart. With each blow the pear shook and shook and shivered, its fruit flying in all directions. Then it fell with a thud embracing the earth below. Earth, mother earth, the cursed mother whose womb not only nourishes her children but also serves as their mass grave. An enraged sun, the celestial eye—witness, blazed hot with all its fury. He would have detached himself from the sky had someone's powerful arms not kept him in place. Their highways crumbling, the furry creatures scurried on the ground like tenants thrown out of their rented apartment without prior notice by the landlord. The spiky lemon wondered what purpose his short existence had served—a solitary survival with neither the koel befriending him nor the crow. But what had he done to earn the animosity of men? For him these last thoughts were more painful than the physical blows he was suffering. The giants watched the whole drama of devastation from their high position. But this time they did not shed leaves. They were so angry and shocked that they could not control themselves. And so they lifted their feet embedded in the soil, quaking the earth below, to punish the madmen. Seeing the strange phenomenon the scared men darted for cover. The giants almost walked a few steps before they realized that they had uprooted themselves. The colossal bodies of the giants crashed and piled up above those of the others. The crow kept hovering and crying and cawing helplessly.

Heaps of dry leaves began to be piled up with green ones. The green ones felt cheated the same way as someone who has paid for the balcony is made to sit in the upper stall. The grass lay crushed and enmeshed with the soil below but did not complain this time. Their spirit of complaining had been trampled over.

The men sat down to cut the wood into sizeable logs then bundled and stacked each piece and carried away the dead. They then gathered the leftover chips of wood, leaves and stubs and set the place on fire. It was such a relief. A whole day's hard work, struggle, sweating had borne fruit. A mammoth task had been accomplished.

The fire spread quickly, engulfing each nook and corner, stifling all traces of life in the garden. The embers glowed red hot in the darkness of the night as the smoke kept rising carrying all anguish and torment upwards. What remained was ash, lots of dry, grey, mute, lifeless ash. When the wind happened to pass by, she sat over the burnt fence and observed a few moments of silence as homage to the departed ones.

But the crow, till this day, rummages the charred remains, hoping to find some clue of the whereabouts of his bosom friend and the good old days together spent.

Up on the Terrace

The terrace of the building was always a place buzzing with activity or rather inactivity in the cold winter season. Now whether it was the bitter chill that drove the housewives beyond the confines of the four walls or whether the season served a mere pretext for the women to get together was difficult to tell for the matter concerned women's mind which anyway is a forbidden territory that even the gods dare not pervade.

Meeta and Tara were busy rolling out papads and shaping out vadis, while Uma would place them very deftly and gingerly over a neatly spread sheet. Antara was running her fingers through the diced raw mangoes evenly laid out over the water tanks. Rashi was wringing the clothes and hanging them over the wash line. Only Hira lay supine over the chatai, her just washed wet white hair beginning to dry in the sun. Hira's face was starting to stiffen with the ineptitude of the housewives around. She was ready to forgive Rashi for wringing the sweaters despite her advice, for Rashi was young, although she wondered what a dandy she would make of her family members with loose sweaters; she was also ready to forgive Antara for running her fingers so often through the raw mangoes, again in violation of her counsel, though she wondered how sour and spoilt the pickle would taste; but she was in no mood to forgive Meeta, Tara and Uma, the older of the lot, for not heeding her recipe for just the right amount of spices to be kneaded in the papads and vadis. Thank heavens, Hira had no trouble with Rashi's little daughter Kanya playing with her dolls nearby and that too because she had had no chance to codify the rules of play.

Occasionally the child went up to the old woman to get her doll's arm fixed in the socket and as a token of appreciation shared her candies with her, so now both of them had reddish orange tongues. Meeta was quick to point out to the others, "Look, now doesn't Hira look like a grand old witch?" The others grinned from ear to ear.

"Did you read the morning papers today?" Uma spoke while still doing her job.

"No, my husband does that for me every morning." Meeta beamed in.

"No, what I meant was did you not hear of the convict who's run away?" Uma informed.

"Yes the one whom the police are chasing." It was Rashi, walking up to the trio, "And I have heard they've even declared a reward for catching him."

Antara ambled her way to the group, taking her fingers off her mangoes much to the delight of Hira. The drowsiness induced by the cozy sun and her doll's swiveling arm kept the oldest and the youngest from joining the rolling pin conference of the housewives. Bright sunshine had swathed everything in its brilliance. Light had displaced darkness of the past cold night from each nook and corner of the terrace. There was no room for shades and shadows. The whitewashed walls reflected and added to the glow. The fog and haze of early morning that had caused poor visibility had vanished without a trace. The potent rays of the sun had set the mood for the day— clear and lucid.

Uma had more to share, "Strange how a fellow chained so heavily to his cell managed to escape?"

"What crime had he committed," questioned Tara.

"Must have been some gory tale of murder and blood. Oh, I didn't bother to read." Rashi spoke settling down over a low bench.

"Violence and blood, ah! I just can't stand them," cried Antara.

"Why would you?" piercing came the voice of Meeta.

"What are you trying to suggest?" Antara seemed to have caught the sting in Meeta's tone.

"Trying to suggest? Oh why would I when everyone around knows what I mean. Come on now haven't we heard glass bottles breaking and your screams in the middle of the night, night after night after night. Even now this bandage around your palm speaks volumes about the gory tales of the past night."

Antara was touched to the quick. She wanted to retort. But when insult is added to injury, it has a strange anesthetic affect over the senses and a very numb Antara simply walked away from the group, tears rushing to her rescue, spreading a thin film of haze over her eyes, occluding her view of the shamelessly rude world around. Sensitive Rashi ran up to Antara to comfort her while Meeta carried on with her chattering, "Had I been in her place I would have simply walked out of the marriage. Not a night's rest."

"Is walking out that easy Meeta?" said Tara shaping the vadis.

"I would have." Meeta appeared adamant.

"Oh come on Meeta, who in the entire neighborhood has not heard your sobs when your children show so much disrespect to you." Uma patted Meeta on the shoulder. A very humbled Meeta carried on with rolling papads albeit with a disgruntled look on her face.

"Chained my dear, chained are we to the cells of our domesticity." The vadis in Tara's hands were acquiring the flavours of philosophy.

The commotion at the terrace had not escaped aged Hira's attention who obviously did not owe the sallowness of her hair entirely to the sun. Her only apprehension this time though was that the women ought not to be talking while preparing eatables. Leaving Rashi to the care of her raw mangoes Antara headed to attend to her chores back home.

"Clothes don't dry in the tiny balconies that we have been provided with and it's so tiring carrying them all the way up here," spoke Rashi walking up to the group.

"Dark, dingy homes, not a ray of light ever penetrates through their length and breadth and even if the rays ever try Mrs. Bhalla's bed sheets loom large from her balcony eclipsing all light and warmth." Meeta was not going to spare this chance of ridiculing Mrs. Bhalla.

"Much like the cells of a jail," chuckled Uma.

"Rashi, how's your progress at the painting classes?" asked Tara.

"Painting, well I couldn't manage going so far for the classes and then rushing back home for household chores as you see now Kanya has started going to school. Responsibilities and duties of the family circle leave no room for hobbies," smiled Rashi.

"And there's more coming," fondly patting Rashi's belly Uma continued, "Tara you are lucky you have no kids to look after, and that leaves you with the luxury of indulging in what you may prefer."

"Luxury, my foot. Whole year round she is at the receiving end of her in-laws comments for being issueless and you call that luxury." Tara was thankful to Meeta for sparing her the ordeal of answering that one.

"Complaining, complaining as if they were serving a sentence. Ah, these women," muttered Hira.

"Do you think this woman dozing off over the chatai also has or ever had any qualms about familial matters and conjugal crises." The housewives were set pondering at Uma's observation.

"Hmm, seasoned! Served her term pretty long; I am sure she's been tamed to the point of no return." Even as others nodded in affirmation to Meeta's remark the white haired over the chatai winked and made herself more comfortable at her sunny spot. The cozy sun lulled her to sleep and then she did not notice how time elapsed.

Dark clouds had started gathering swiftly and hastily as if they were in a hurry to dim all light and radiance. Bold outstretched arms of clouds were firming their grip over the sun, devouring it and pulling it deep into a swirling flood. The whitewashed walls appeared to have connived with murk to run the shadow play of clothes hung over the line. The arms and torsos twisted and contorted, now advancing and now retreating with the current of air. Nooks and corners were the first ones to plunge into obscurity. But it was a fire shot that awakened Hira. She was still rubbing her eyes when she noticed Antara come hurrying to the terrace.

"Hear that! The afternoon bulletin said he's been sighted in our area" announced Antara as she started gathering the ends of her sheet that carried the raw mangoes.

"Wow! Let him come. I'll straightaway catch hold of him and hand him over to the police and claim the reward. Meeta! Tara! Imagine, end of laborious days of rolling and drying papads and vadis and carrying them over to that miser Gupta's store. Ugh! How I detest it when he counts down the coins over my palm as if I were a beggar." Uma was wild with excitement.

Meeta and Tara could not remain unaffected and even started to calculate their share of the booty to be, although the advancing rough weather and the gunshot had panicked them causing them to wind up their business for the day.

"Let me lay my hands over the wretch," Antara shouted tightening her bandage clenched in her teeth, "and I'll show how it is when a woman takes to beating." The other wives were amazed at an emboldened Antara.

Rashi began taking the wet clothes off the wash line. Clasping her doll tightly in one hand Kanya held her mother tight with the other. "Mama, are they playing thief—police?"

"Yes dear."

"What will they do to the thief once they catch him?"

"They will handcuff him and chain him."

"Where will they take him?" Now Rashi was getting irked by her child's unending queries.

"They will put him back in the jail!" she shouted.

"How does a jail look like?"

"Dark, dingy, no light and no freedom! He stays there tied for a lifetime! Do you get that and now dare you ask me another question." By the time she finished speaking she had the terrace reverberating with her voice and the housewives shell shocked. The child was too terrified to ask anything else.

Just then there was some clinking noise behind the water tanks. Someone had leapt over from the adjoining wall. The wives stared at each other in amazement. Overhead, the dark clouds were thundering and menacing as they marched across the sky, barring entry to rays that struggled to wade through.

Heavy footsteps could be heard approaching the terrace from the stairs. It was the police.

"Seen a man, a shaggy fellow? The convict? Did he land up here?" The men in uniform were panting at the threshold aiming their pistols even as their eyes searched and searched. Silence ensued for a moment. Hira walked up to the men folding her chatai and bundling it under her arm. "Seen? What seen? We are all honourable women minding our business here. Drying papads, vadis and our clothes and ourselves. No man ever dare turn up here. Let me find one and I'll roll him over like a papad." With a twinkle in her eyes, she spoke uninterrupted.

"Come on boys, rush downstairs, we've landed at the wrong place." The men scurried off.

Parole over, the inmates too descended down to their cells.

The Cherished Photo

Every time he sat at the sweets shop sipping his cup of tea, he looked at the well garlanded, well framed huge pictures of Lubhaya's deceased parents. His eyes moistened and he experienced a strange sense of satisfaction as he observed Lubhaya light incense sticks in front of the pictures, then kneel down in reverence, mumble a little prayer and only then sit down at the counter for the day's business. This was a daily ritual for Lubhaya. Each time Lalaji observed this ritual he wondered if his progeny would ever light incense sticks and kneel in front of his photo, when they wished him dead even as he was alive—progeny that did not treat him with decency, progeny that did not care to know whether he had his meals on time or had them at all.

But when people die, things are different. Everyone mourns the dead, irrespective of whether they had any grudges against the one who departed. The society is kinder to the dead. The children anyway missed their parents when they died and often narrated the incidents and time they spent together. But all this were possible only if he too had such a grand photo of himself. The ill-gotten had never cared to get him clicked and he knew this would serve as an excuse for not kneeling before him after he was dead.

As days passed, he got even more determined to get himself clicked—photographed in grand style. A humble wish to be remembered as a respectable man-a man who attired his strong healthy body in clean well-ironed clothes. He refused to identify with his present day miserable self in soiled worn out clothes.

"Where to Lalaji in such hurry? And wait a minute! If my memory does not fail me and which does not by the grace of the Pir who rests by the pipal tree, the last time I saw you wearing this fine suit was on your son's wedding", Juni said giving her peculiar one-sided smile.

Lalaji had seen Juni coming from the opposite direction. Who could tell from where she was coming or where to she was heading? He knew that he might have succeeded in wading through the bazaar thus far ignoring everyone's remarks, regarding his unusual appearance; he could not, even if he tried, evade this shrill voiced middle aged woman. He had feared being intercepted by Juni all this while but the more you fear fears, more they turn true. Whether she was a widow or she ever got married or she ever had any living soul in this world to call her own, no one ever knew. But Juni knew everyone through and through. She made a living out of it. All those who had an ear for gossip would invite her, all those wishing to know how others thought of them called her. She was the eyes and ears of the entire village, but not its conscience. They said she was born without one. Village men stared at delicate damsels as they passed by but their heads shook when Juni crossed them. For her sight pierced through them and pricked their conscience.

Lalaji stopped, cleared his throat and then entered the nearest shop without saying a word. It was not in Juni's veins to be rebuffed. While a shaky Lalaji waited inside for her to move on, longing to reach the photographer, he did not notice the shop he had entered. But Juni eagerly noted. It was Roopchand Sunar's jewellery shop. She had found the breaking news, the most sensational gossip around!

"That aged Lala, yes the one whose house is at the bend of the street, yes, yes, you've guessed it right, the one whose wife died, he's the one", she whispered loudly into Ram Lal, the tea vendor's ears and he offered her a hot cup of ginger flavored tea. There from Juni proceeded to Veeran's house and from there to Pushpa's. It was indeed a hectic day but by the end of it Juni had earned a whole two kilograms of jaggery, wheat flour, some corn and a huge amount of appreciation for her services.

"Hmm! I too wondered why he was admiring himself in the mirror this morning", said Rano, the daughter-in-law. "Now we must summon the village headman and get the property legally divided. We must call up the younger brother from the other village. There is going to be a third one we will have to share this property with. Oh! Who could be a more heartless parent than this man", she cried even as her cries grew from normal to hysterical. The other women in the village had started gathering. They offered their dupattas to Rano to wipe her big tears with. They offered her a cool glass of water but she would not drink.

"Juni, you yourself saw it?" asked one.

"Oh! I swear in the name of the Pir who rests by the pipal tree, I did."

"Even I saw him the other day gifting something to that widow; why the one who lives in the mud house", remarked another.

"Gifting? What did you say gift! Oh! Look at that broken kitchen window. He never gave us any money even to mend it and the poor cat keeps getting cursed for prowling in the kitchen." At this Rano sent out a louder wail.

"I have seen times grow from bad to worse. I pray for the coming generations. God knows what not they will have to witness," said another well-wisher, folding her hands and shutting her eyes. Rano's husband was quick to arrive accompanied by some wise men of the village.

Lalaji was too pleased with himself as he came out of the photo studio. He had selected a golden frame. But the photographer said it would take sometime for he needed to work on the grand picture. He proudly put his hands in his pockets and jingled the coins. Yes, now only coins jingled. But those pockets had seen prosperous days. What would an old man do with cash, carry it to his pyre? Old age is the time when man must cast away the veil of maya—illusion; at least, so said the pundit at the temple. That the aged man in his present circumstances could not afford even an inch of the veil was beyond the scope of religious texts.

They all waited for Lalaji to return home. But they could wait at leisure only till dusk whence they returned to attend to their half done chores and daily business of life. Before leaving, they all assured Rano and her husband that they were not alone in their hour of tragedy.

People switched on their electric bulbs. Their village was lucky enough to have electricity supply. The candidate from their constituency had kept his promise. After all they had turned up in huge numbers to cast their votes in his favour. Electrifying are the promises of democracy!

Rano was serving food to her husband when Lalaji walked in through the door. His retreat through the bazaar had acquainted him of Juni's mischief. He didn't look up and with his gaze fixed on the floor, he headed straight to his room. He would give no explanations till they asked. And they were determined not to ask. Let the old man have his meals from wherever he could!

Through the long night, tired and hungry lay wounded senility condemned to darkness which even the electric bulbs of democracy failed to dispel. At such times it was always the memory of his mother that kept him company. Mother—who went out of the way to please her child. Mother—who willingly bore the heat and sweat in the kitchen for long hours to cook her son's favourite dishes. Mother—who served hot steaming food to her son before she served it to anyone else. Mother—who would rather feed the dogs with last night's leftovers than serve them to her son. But an unloved old man is a stray dog. Stray dogs—who have no fixed hours for eating food, who eat whenever food is given, nay thrown at them.

With no follow up, the sensational news died down. Juni was clueless. She could provide no inputs to sustain the gossip for long. The villagers saw no imminent threat to the materialistic concerns of the harrowed family. Even Lalaji's behaviour did not help to poke the fire.

He attended the morning and evening prayers at the temple. Young women looked at him with suspicion. Men walked a step ahead or behind, never keeping pace with him.

But as days passed by, Lalaji stopped going to the temple to offer prayers. Few days later, he even stopped moving out of his room. Now he would not leave the bed either. He snapped the chords with the world that had turned a blind eye to him, in the reverse order in which he had tied them.

Juni was sitting in the open verandah sipping the hot cup of tea that Rano had served her. Munching the hard shakkerpaare, she cursed her falling teeth. She was telling her about the spirits that roamed the fields at night, when the postman came up with a huge parcel. Rano received the parcel and as Juni waited anxiously, Rano eagerly clipped the tags and tore off the wrapping paper. There emerged a huge picture cased in golden frame. The gentleman in the picture wore the same fine suit that Juni had last seen Lalaji in. Below the picture were inscribed the words, 'Lala Kirpa Ram'. Rano knew what to do with the picture. It was just the right size to fit into the kitchen window exactly from where the cat sneaked in.

Vegetables

One fine afternoon just after her children were back from school, Mrs. Verma had an urge to eat green chilies. She usually avoided chilies in her diet but that day she felt that if she did not have some she might just break all the furniture, the glassware, the window-panes and all that was in the house amenable to the laws of destruction. She headed straight to the refrigerator and not finding any she rummaged the cartons in the kitchen. But to her dismay she found that there weren't any chilies in the entire house. The vegetable vendor! Yes! She thought she must wait and watch out for a stray vegetable vendor. What might be the cause of her weird craving? Perhaps it was a deficiency of vitamin C. Was it? Or was she trying to divert her mind from the last night's scuffle with her husband whence he had charged her for being 'such a stale rather rotten piece of vegetable.' She waited restlessly to hear the call of a vendor. "Fresh, green, leafy vegetables!" She jumped the moment she heard the words she was most anxiously waiting to hear and rushed to the street. On reaching the spot she found that she was not the only one to have been waiting, for the vendor was already surrounded by several other women presumably from the same neighborhood. Making her way through the crowd she began filling her basket with chilies. But while she was doing all this she sensed that someone was closely watching her movements. She instantly looked up and saw that it was none other than the vendor-a tall, shabby, plain-looking vendor. Vendors are in the habit of watching keenly, lest the buyer walks away without bothering to pay, she thought and carried on with her work.

That evening while Mrs. Verma was cooking in her kitchen, her attention repeatedly wavered to the green chillies lying in the basket and then on to the person she had purchased them from. There was something in the way he looked at her that she could not forget. She had not been used to being looked at in that manner since her college days.

As days went by Mrs. Verma discovered that her stock of green chilies failed to keep pace with her urge to eat them. Coming days saw her turn in to a frequent buyer of green chilies. In addition to chilies she even started buying the rest of her vegetables from the vendor. A very health conscious Mr. Verma was only too delighted to eat meals cooked from fresh green vegetables. The seemingly monotonous act of buying vegetables gave Mrs. Verma the opportunity to know other women in the neighborhood. Mrs. Verma even managed to befriend a very cordial Mrs. Bhalla.

The plain looking shabby vegetable vendor was not the only one to venture into the neighborhood. There were many more of them. But the women preferred him to the rest for he was different. He was one of those men who had managed to cross over to the lonely shores of femininity walking the tight rope of communication cables. His vegetables were not greener than those of the others, nor were they fresher, nor did he offer them at any discounted rates. Women flocked him for he had struck a chord with them. When Mrs. Sharma enquired whether he had any tomatoes, he would say, "But not as red as the cheeks of Her Highness." And whenever Mrs. Bhalla enquired about okra he would shake his gunny bags and hold out a handful saying that he had some that were only as slender as Mrs. Bhalla's fingers. And when Mrs. Chopra asked him to pass on some bitter gourd, "Oh! May curse befall the day when God made such bitter things for so sweet creatures as women," he would lament. Mr. Gupta might have left for office without taking note of his wife but the vendor never missed pointing out to Mrs. Gupta that that day she had got up from the wrong side of her bed. One glance at Mrs. Verma and the vendor would shout out, "O what an evil night it must have been that denied an angel her share of sleep." Above all, the clarion call that he gave out to the women as he sounded his arrival was, 'fresh, green, leafy vegetables.' There was so much dignity, almost divinity in this form of salutation. .

The vendor had mastered the art that housewives secretly desired their husbands to have some rudimentary knowledge of. No doubt, the housewives waited an agonizing wait for his shrill voice to pierce into the silence of their boring afternoons. They spent such long time in selecting the vegetables that they did not even spend in cooking them. He told jokes that were anything but funny and the wives laughed, he recited half forgotten lines of couplets and the wives applauded, he simply opened his mouth and the wives giggled, he smiled and the wives blushed.

Poor husbands! If only they knew how badly they were rated as compared to the shabby vegetable vendor. But what use is the knowledge that makes a dinner unappetizing?

Mr. Verma particularly found the vendor to be a nasty fellow. Why shouldn't he? The way he parked his cart loaded with vegetables right in front of his car just when he was about to leave for his office was very exasperating for Mr.Verma. It was only on repeated honking that the scruffy fellow would budge an inch. Mrs. Verma found the spectacle too flattering as she looked out of her kitchen window.

The wives in the neighborhood started having unusually good mood. They complained less and worked harder. What disconcerted the husbands was that any reference to them of being stale or rotten failed to bring them to tears. What alarmed the husbands most was that the peeling of onions also failed to activate their lachrymal glands. To hedge against any further damage, Mr. Verma, as also the other husbands, instantly took a break from all their official duties and accompanied their wives to the shopping mall and forced them into buying the latest fashion wear, the newly launched shades of lipsticks and nail varnishes. After that they took them for candlelight dinner at which, kneeling down, they even apologized to them for having neglected them for so long due to the burden of their official duties.

What started perplexing the vendor was the deviant behavior of the wives who instead of paying their full attention to him now kept discussing their husbands and to what extent they went in order to please them. He felt as if the women were drifting away. Had his spell broken? Was his incantation losing power? He began doling out green chilies and coriander leaves for free but the drifting did not cease. He tried ignoring the ladies altogether for full five days hoping ignore to achieve what attention could not, but the drift continued. He tried all means to divert the attention of the wives to the brighter, greener, fresher side of life, only to discover that they had drifted beyond reach. When Mrs.Verma also joined the ranks of Mrs. Sharma, Mrs. Chopra, Mrs. Bhalla and the rest of them all did the vendor feel within him the rise of the spirit of an Emperor threatened with the loss of his imperial harem.

Days passed, then a week, then weeks together but the vendor did not come. What happened, where he went no one could find out. The husbands, on their part, could not afford to play a poodle to their better-halves all the year round. They lapsed into their old habits.

The hot sultry mornings and noons once again saw the wives straining their ears to catch a shrill note of the vendor's voice, but the vendor did not come. Mrs. Sharma even swore at the kitty party to have heard a faint voice quite like that of the vendor's but others knew it was a mere illusion. All the husbands noted the sudden onset of depression in their wives but were clueless over the cause. The wives were slowly but surely losing interest in all their daily activities. The despondency of the wives was becoming unbearable for the husbands.

The days had lost their brightness, their greenery and their freshness for the wives. The boring emptiness of their lives had crept back. They had been displaced from their exalted position by the evil hands of unfriendly forces.

It was just another day as a heart-broken Mrs. Verma began cleaning her refrigerator. There were quite a few withered vegetables that needed sorting out. She could not get herself to believe that such a commonplace activity as clearing up stale vegetables could charge her up emotionally. Suddenly she felt a gush of wind blow at her, pushing away the stray locks of hair gathered over her forehead and giving her a thorough shake. She felt as if she heard someone call out her name. No, not the one others called her by but the one she identified herself with, 'Fresh, Green, Leafy Vegetable.' She strained her ears beyond human capacities to hear some illusory notes of the fugitive vendor's voice.

There was actually a sound heard. A familiar sound. Shrill? Sure shrill! Over and above all other sounds. The faint shrill was growing louder every moment. His voice spelt the end of tormenting days of the wives. There was indeed light, nay sound, at the end of the tunnel. They ran barefoot. They ran sans their baskets. They ran sans the cash. They ran in ecstasy. They ran as fast as they could. They stormed the vendor with queries. They made so much noise that the burrowing animals left their burrows to check whether all was fine with the world outside. "One by one, my fair maidens," the vendor winked at the ladies. "Oh really nothing, I just went fishing for some fresher, greener, vegetables to help you keep young forever. Oh, I missed you so much myself." The vendor blushed as the ladies were only one step short of tearing down his attire. Mrs. Sharma almost fainted. Mrs. Chopra could hardly catch hold of her breath. The vendor gave a huge smile flashing his golden tooth. "Aa aa, a gold tooth," chorused the wives. The vendor ran his fingers through his hair. "A new hairstyle!" cheered the wives. The vendor looked over his shoulder searching for Mrs. Verma but she was nowhere around.

He quickly picked up two lemons and two green chilies and squeezed them with his hands, then closed his eyes and mumbled something. The effect was instantaneous. Something in Mrs. Verma melted and she felt pulled by some mesmeric force to the vegetable vendor in the street. She occupied her place among the several others gathered around him, smiled and started sorting out green chilies. The vendor winked for his magic had worked.

Watchman

The buntings and balloons that Kunal's doting aunts had hung all over the place were coming off. They had to. When revelry lasts so long, someone has to remind the party enthusiasts it is time to wrap up. The noisy clattering and clanking of cutlery continued as food connoisseurs relished the dishes so daintily prepared by the aunts themselves. Adoring aunts realized the importance of homemade food for the motherless lad who seldom had the opportunity to mingle with the family circle, staying far away at the boarding school whole year round. But this time round the high school boy had arranged a get together for all those relatives whose faces he still reckoned in the family album-happy faces of happier times spent together. One face that flashed across his mind was the charming face of his mother. But the memory was painful for it also reminded him of the turmoil that followed her suicide and his being hurriedly sent off to the boarding school. One nagging question that he could never get rid of was 'why, just why did she have to leave.' Perhaps the aunts also sensed his sorrow for every now and then they came over to give him a big burly affectionate hug. The merry making, the chitter—chatter, the aroma of fried food, the loud music and dancing constantly diverted his attention to the joyous mood around.

There was one, just one person whom Kunal regretted having invited to the gathering—his granny. Now he was beginning to realize that there are some people who can neither live happily themselves nor allow others around to gain some measure of happiness. The old woman had kept sitting stiffly over her seat ever since she came, refusing to become a part and parcel of the gathering and refusing also to allow anyone around to ignore her. She was not amused by the carousing, alright, but she did not even pretend; even if it meant pleasing her grandson she was meeting so long after. The vibes that she sent had forced Ankit and his girlfriend to carry on with their dancing in the next room. Let alone complimenting the aunts for their efforts, the grumpy old lady had shown no inclination to even taste the food. No wonder aunt Trishla kept lamenting, 'just who had prepared the guest list; someone should have consulted me at least.' Kunal was amazed at the angelic disposition of aunt Chitra who had been kind enough to give company and play host to the grouchy spoilsport even if it meant sitting silently next to her. Though the number of times she crossed and uncrossed her legs could have led anyone to believe she was bored to the limits and just about to get up and leave. He was equally appreciative of his father who sat composed opposite granny on the sofa, giving his cheerful smile to the guests.

"Will someone please turn off the music? Oh it's getting late, really." It was uncle Om's authoritative voice. The command was most obediently obeyed. But how could dancing carry on without the music.

So now there was very little incentive left for the younger lot to stay. "Go and see them off dear," with a pat over the shoulder from his father, an unwilling Kunal went on to do something that he most disliked. There standing at the gate and bidding adieu to his friends and cousins he wished the party had never got over. Throughout the day, narrating his experiences at the boarding school to his friends and reminiscing the days he had spent with them at the local school, collecting the addresses of the ones who had left town, talking in hushed tones when it came to the girls in the neighborhood, sharing his concerns regarding his career plans, had not been enough.

He stood there waving at the gate long after they had left, lost in his thoughts unaware of the darkness that had set in with fog close at its heels. The cold wintry chill caused him some discomfort but he kept standing there for a while staring at the path that was not even discernible. All was quiet, not a sound, only the distant laughter and conversation of his aunts and uncles. Suddenly he felt as if he heard something. As the sound grew louder he realized someone was approaching him through the dark pathway shaking him out of his reverie. Looking hard he could make the outline of a short statured stocky fellow. Kunal almost gave a cry of horror as the fellow beamed his torchlight at him. It was the watchman. "Out boy! Too late and cold to be out." Kunal moved back a step as the Gurkha gave him his toothy smile and tapped at the gate with his baton.

Kunal retraced his steps to the noisy living room. The warmth of the room made him realize how numb with cold his hands had become. Rubbing his hands he gazed at the room as if he was entering it for the first time. A strange disenchantment had taken hold of him. There in a corner sat his uncles discussing the municipal elections. Forming a large cluster sat his aunts some of whom having started late were not yet done with their dinner. Aunt Chitra could be spotted yawning and sliding her foot back and forth in her high heeled shoes. He looked at the old woman sitting silently next to her and wondered if it was not time for her to leave. After all the fog would only grow dense as the night advanced and at her age one ought to be in bed by now. But Kunal scolded himself for being so concerned about someone who cared not an iota about him. By now he was convinced that the stiff woman's sitting there so dumb in that posture was meant to punish them in some way. Punish them perhaps for being alive, for continuing to live even after her daughter had ceased to. Punish them perhaps for merry-making when they ought to mourn.

Aunt Trishala noticed him standing there and fondly stroking back the hair over his forehead, she dragged him to a place in the centre of the room. There seating him over a chair she sat down beside him. "What is it you are thinking about?" she asked. Not ready with an answer he fumbled and blurted "The watchman." "Ah, the watchman." Overhearing the conversation was uncle Om. "Good god, our watchman is a lazy fellow. He turns up only in the first week of every month when he has to collect his dues." "Yes and the threat of burglars always looms large at places where the watchman fails to keep guard," aunt Trishala spoke thoughtfully. "How's the watchman here?" uncle Om queried Kunal's father. "Good, good, quite regular," he replied. But the uncle seemed to have given a deeper thought to the subject. "I wonder how much you can trust these fellows. They might actually connive with the burglars and assist them in carrying out their operations. After all they have all the information regarding each house in a locality." Seeing others engaged in a topic not to his liking, Kunal whispered in Trishala's ear, "Don't you think it's time for granny to leave?" Trishala gave a mysterious smile. "It's up to her Kunal. We can't ask a guest to leave like that." Kunal nodded reluctantly.

As the night proceeded, the fog grew thicker and thicker. The winter chill could be felt even by looking at it through the window. Kunal wished to be in the coziness of his room. He was yawning. So were his aunts and uncles many of whom had started leaving by now. But there was one person who refused to budge from her seat. His granny, of course. Kunal's sympathies were with aunt Chitra who albeit a guest herself, was playing the perfect host to the stubborn one sitting next to her. The silence of the night was repeatedly interrupted by the watchman on the beat as he tapped at the gates and the doors as if deliberately breaking the soundness of people's sleep to enlighten them in the darkness of the night that those who sleep so deeply and so care freely, run the risk of being robbed the most.

Trishala looked at the clock and decided it was time to leave. Almost all the friends and relatives had left and now there was no point in staying back. She gestured to Om to ready the car. But before leaving she walked up to Chitra and offered to drop her at her place. "Chitra, at this hour it is going to be difficult for you to even find a taxi." Chitra looked at granny. "Yes come along, come along. Trishala's been kind enough to have offered us a lift." Saying this granny rose from her seat and holding Chitra tightly by the arm nearly dragged her to the door. Kunal watched how roughly and rudely his granny was handling someone who had been so compassionate towards her through the entire day. He felt hurt at the stone heartedness of someone so closely related to him. When aunt Trishala was showering him with hugs and kisses before parting he wondered why his granny had not even cared to wish him a simple adieu. The father son duo stood waving at the last of their guests. The car slowly vanished behind the thick curtain of fog.

Even as his father went away, Kunal kept standing in the doorway staring at the cold dark night. He must have been standing there for a while when he noticed a figure emerge out of the hazy curtain. He sensed a motherly figure walking towards him. Perhaps it was his mother. He gave a cry of joy and rushed forward. It was aunt Trishala beaming at him.

"I left my purse here, Kunal. Just rushed back to collect it. We had not even gone past the bend in the road. By the way what are you doing standing here at the door?" Kunal nodded and followed her to the table where her purse lay. As she opened it and checked to make sure nothing was missing, Kunal inched closer, "Aunt, w-why d-do y—you think mom left us. You promised to tell me when I was a grown up lad. Am am I n-not grown up now." He stammered but managed to complete his sentence. His aunt smiled and held his innocent face in her hand. "Chitra, it was Chitra who had vitiated the whole atmosphere. Why else do you think your granny kept sitting glued to her through the day." Kissing him on the cheek she disappeared as swiftly as she had arrived. The boy stood agape at the door. In the distance could be heard the thumping and banging of the watchman's baton—watchman who disrupted the night and guarded it.

Hunt

"Phew! What a creature!" Chuckled Sahil on seeing Rita enter the venue for the 'Treasure Hunt' contest on her rickety moped. "Straight from the shelves of a curio—shop," Ronnie seconded Sahil as both the boys posed themselves confidently in front of their flashy SUV. The contest was an added attraction this year at the annual carnival of Chandigarh being held at the Leisure Valley. There was a huge rush at the organizers'-desk for collecting the I-cards as the participants jostled past the craftsmen busy setting up their stalls and performers rehearsing their parts.

With the striking of the gong the chief guest declared the contest open and the first cue flashed across the mobile phones of the contestants. The SMS read,

'No ambergris, no myrrh required,
Yet in fragrance you get mired.'

In a city based on the concept of Garden Cities, it was not difficult to surmise that the cue pointed to Asia's largest rose garden, the 'Zakir Rose Garden' located just across the road. It being a sunny winter season, the sixteen hundred odd varieties of roses were in full bloom, beckoning the urban rats to stall their race for a while. Letting out an ear-piercing din, the showy two-wheelers and four-wheelers rolled out raising a huge cloud of smoke and dust. When the dust settled, Rita could still be seen kicking her moped that showed no inclination to start. When the contraption did wheel out on the wide and clean roads of independent India's first planned city, Rita wondered whether she was the hunter or destiny's perennially hunted—down.

What gladdened her heart was the sight of so many co-participants being rounded up and challanned by the Chandigarh traffic police for over-speeding, helmetless driving, triple—riding and so on. But even these scary uniformed men and women, who gave nightmares to the road users, wondered as Rita rode past them, whether a human—dragged—machine, for that is what it appeared to them, fell under their jurisdiction. The sight of Rita riding her antiquated vehicle was so singular in its form that children in a school-bus passing by started shouting, "UFO! UFO!" The cameraman of a local newspaper on the verge of being fired from his job had his position secured with a single flash.

Meanwhile, Sahil and Ronnie had reached the rose garden well ahead of the others and after making an entry in the organizer's register were busy making head and tail of the cue on the cue card.

"Metal—head on a mount,
Footfalls you cannot count,"

Sahil read it aloud. "What do you think Ronnie?" He asked a rather puzzled fellow. "Why, there is a plethora of statues and their dumb heads in the museum and art gallery adjacent to the Leisure Valley. But what I fail to understand is that are the organizers out of their mind to keep us running back and forth over this stretch," the indignation in Ronnie's voice was amply clear. The duo steered their vehicle back to square one. Not spotting the organizer's desk at the gate, they bought entry tickets to the museum to hunt for the elusory metal—head. As precious time ticked on, Sahil told Ronnie not to lose heart for he had read in a book of a person finding treasure right at the place he had started off from.

The second cue found Rita heading straight for the shopping complex at sector 17. "Metal head must refer to the fountain spouting water at the sector 17 plaza. Chandigarh being basically a market for consumer goods, its shopping arcade has innumerable fashion—conscious people visiting it to buy branded apparels, shoes, hand-bags and so on," she reasoned with herself. She was not disappointed as she spotted the organizers ready to hand over the next cue card to her. Eager to open the sealed envelope, her hands fumbled as she looked around the place that every city dweller loved to hang around. The newly built malls at the outskirts of the city had evidently begun to wean away people from here. Rita could sense the thinning of crowds at the various shops where once securing even a foothold was a privilege. The tempting aroma of the popcorns popping out of the popcorn machines made her forget for a while that she was on a mission. She bought herself a pack of popcorns and a twin-flavored softy. Gorging over them she wondered how she could overlook the ritual she had been performing since the times she visited the place holding her mama's finger or perched on her papa's shoulder.

It was their aching feet that compelled Sahil and Ronnie that if they did not give up their wild goose chase in the museum, they might soon pass in to history, only to be pointed at by a visitor exclaiming, "Look, that is how the moron hunter of the twenty-first century looked like." The boys rang up their friends in desperation. The friends realizing that they themselves were way ahead on their pursuit of the third clue had pity on them and directed them to sector 17.

'Blue giants do not frown
As visitors abound from a chilly town.'

That was what the third clue read. The contestants, most of them being university students, always kept themselves well informed of the cultural activities taking place around the city whose own culture was an admixture of the flavours lent to it by the Punjabis, Haryanvis and Himachalis who had settled there. 'Visitors from a chilly town,' they knew for sure referred to the Kashmiri dance group which had come to perform at the Tagore Theatre. Even Ronnie jumped with joy when he told Sahil that he remembered having seen a burly security guard in blue uniform at the theatre. Sahil could not help marveling at his luck that had bestowed the friendship of such a genius on him.

It was only Rita who was heading on a different route at the sluggish pace that her moped could manage. Whenever she stopped at the lights point, the city ladies sitting in style in their chauffeur-driven cars wondered why a young girl was going the whole hog spoiling her matrimonial prospects seated on a despicable vehicle that blatantly declared the economic status of its owner.

Riding on and on Rita found herself amidst the imposing buildings of the northern sectors. She gave an envious look at the spacious houses around. "Life in the thinly populated northern part of the city seems so relaxed and easy as compared to the cramped existence in the flats of the southern sectors," she sighed. "If only I had a lot of money could I afford . . . . . . ," her train of thoughts was disrupted by speedily moving cars and motorcycles of the other participants. Some of them had the audacity of running their vehicles parallel to hers and making faces at her. "Want a lift babe," was the jeering remark passed at her by Sahil and Ronnie who had zoomed on the right track, courtesy their SUV, after paying a futile visit to the theatre. She feigned not to have seen them or heard them either, notwithstanding the terror that gripped her heart. "Father always says that 'impossible is a word in the dictionary of fools' and fool is who I am to have dared to aspire to compete where others are not only better equipped but also smart enough if not smarter than I am."

Gigantic trees with sprawling canopies stood on both sides of the road as mute witnesses to the struggle of a young girl as an echo of the struggle of the young city trying to carve a niche for herself with barely her own self to rely on. Tears began rolling down her hot red cheeks. She was angry and she was feeling terribly helpless. Her first instinct was to abandon the hunt and hide herself behind the huge trunks of the trees around. Even here her moped played the spoilsport as its shoe-break refused to bring the whole thing to a stop as per the desire of its rider. As the rattling-clattering moped approached the Governor House, its guards immediately took positions behind the canons, ready to repel so sudden an attack on the most important symbol of state authority in the Union Territory. Seeing simple lass atop a heap of rolling junk, the bemused guards retired to their posts. But they made it a point to inform the intelligence agencies to keep track of a weird being moving under suspicious circumstances.

Rita alighted from her moped at the most picturesque spot of the city-the Sukhna Lake. The blue tinted foothills of a branch of the Himalayas stood in the backdrop of a lake that was regularly supplied by small water channels running down the foothills. In the sixty-one year old history of the city, each winter the lake had played host to a variety of migratory birds who flew thousands of miles to keep their date with the City Beautiful—a sobriquet that found its full justification in these salubrious surroundings. Nature lovers and tourists could be seen thronging the place, their cameras working overtime to capture the city's beauty and take it back home.

On reaching the organizer's desk, Rita was hesitant in extending her hand to receive the cue-card. Her spirits had gone abysmally low and she saw no point in pursuing a goal for which she was so hopelessly equipped. The organizer on duty also seemed in no hurry to hand her over the card for he had himself misplaced the pack and was hurriedly looking for it among his belongings. Rita was about to retrace her steps when she noticed her tormentors pedaling their boats in the lake. "Here they are!" The organizer cried out on managing to locate the cards. "Hare they are indeed," repeated Rita as she was reminded of an over-confident hare who always thought himself to be smarter than the slow paced tortoise. She smiled at the organizer, thanked him and clenching her cue card in between her teeth, rejoined her trail of the treasure.

'Discarded was the fuse,
Bangles of myriad hues,
Shards of china to amuse,'

read the message printed on the card. Ronnie told Sahil to concentrate on pedaling the boat and leave the deciphering of the clue to him. "Here, first of all let me underline the important words in the card and which according to me are 'fuse, bangles and china'. Look here Sahil, this one clearly points to the crowded market at sector 22 where the multitudes of the city go for shopping." "Just like the 'blue giant' pointed at the security guard at the Tagore Theatre?"

Sahil did not try to hide the scorn in his speech. "Chill Sahil, chill! Aren't there bangle shops in 22? Isn't the market flooded with Chinese goods?" "But how do you account for the 'discarded fuse and China with a small c,' bellowed Sahil. "Don't we discard a fuse when it's of no use and as for the small c for China, well, that could just very well be a misprint and in case you don't believe me you can cross check with Aadi," Ronnie defended his stand. "But is he reliable? His interpretation of the previous clue was also wide off the mark," spoke a sulking Sahil. Ronnie shrugged his shoulders. Caught between the horns of dilemma, Sahil called up Aadi who put his call on hold. "Know why Aadi's done this?" Ronnie asked his exasperated friend. "Of course to while away some time before he gets a decisive edge over us." Their legs aching with the fatigue of pedaling, the duo felt like jumping into the lake out of sheer desperation.

Kick-starting her moped Rita was trying to fit the bangles, the fuse and myriad hues into the jigsaw puzzle when a foreign tourist accosted her with a friendly smile. "Mademoiselle, puis-je obtenir un tour s'il vous plaît?"(Ma'am, Can I get a ride please ?) Speaking thus, the Frenchman adjusted himself on the pillion. Rita wanted to refuse for the simple reason that her delicate riding device could not handle the weight of two people. But it was good samaritanism that prevailed for the cue-card clenched between her teeth made any quick refusal impossible. An instant later she found herself double-riding on the road leading away from the lake. "I hope the traffic police do not notice the pillion—rider riding without a helmet," she was murmuring to herself when the Frenchman, shouting over the din of the moped, told her that he was delighted to know that she understood French. "Monsieur," said she, "I owe it to my French connection." "You mean to say that one of your parents belongs to France?" he queried. "No monsieur, it's by virtue of being born and brought up in a city designed by the French architect Le Corbusier." He smiled at being filled with pride at a fellow countryman's achievement. After all, the peculiar architecture of the city with methodically laid buildings looked quite remarkable. "And what's this Rock Garden all about? Rocks are supposed to be barren and to fathom a garden over them seems like a paradox. Strange-a garden of rocks in your city? " He asked her. Instantly the harsh realities of city—life flashed across her 'inward eye' which did not allow her to dwell on the beauty of 'daffodils' like the celebrated poet. "Hmm, garden of rocks to match the stony hardness of urban life," mumbled Rita to herself. "Did you say something," asked the Frenchman. Rita was silent for a while as if lost in grave thoughts. "Are you here on a holiday?" she queried. "Oh yes mademoiselle!" "Then in that case you would want to enjoy yourself and go back home feeling better. What good would it do to you to know that this city too has its fair share of troubles that you are attempting to escape, even if temporarily?" Rita's remark quite confused the foreigner, sensing which Rita donned her role of a good citizen once again. "That garden, created by Nek Chand, is made from the articles of refuse fashioned in to fantastic figures, all thematically laid out," she spoke bringing the moped to a screeching halt. "Here we reach the garden you wanted to visit, I presume." "Oh yes sure, but before I leave I would like to tell you that other than the Eiffel Tower if there is an awe-inspiring metallic wonder on the face of this earth then it is this, it is this, it is this," he spoke, apparently bowled over by the moped, even as a dumbstruck Rita listened, wondering if her moped had rattled any of his bones, especially those of the cranium. Rita was anxious to resume her hunt as soon as possible, for she doubted that the 'myriad hues' of the cue might refer to the colors of the carnival. As the Frenchman turned to cross the road, Rita noticed the organizer's desk outside the Rock Garden and in a moment it flashed across her mind that it was the broken pieces of pottery, glass bangles and electrical items that Nek Chand had used to give concrete shape to his imagination that the cue had all the while been hinting at.

After what seemed like an age, Sahil called up Aadi. Ronnie was surprised when Sahil snapped the call midway. "Why did you do that Sahil? Is there any time to lose now?" He shouted. "Aadi wants to strike a deal," he said. "What deal?"Ronnie was inquisitive to know. "The devil ! He wants us to pay for the recharge of his girlfriend's mobile phone!" While the other contestants were heading for the next destination in their hunt, two bosom friends could be seen searching for a mobile recharge kiosk.

"In a world where they all fight,
His solutions shine so bright,
Peace for the one who by his mantra abides,
There is water on three sides,"

Rita mumbled to herself as she folded back the envelope handed over to her. She knew for sure who it could be, whose message of peace was so relevant to the times she was living in.

By the time she reached the main road, the floats designed by the students of the arts college had begun rolling out leading to a traffic jam. The vehicular traffic was being redirected to other routes to make way for the brilliantly colored floats. The enormous figures appeared to be walking straight out of the pages of a book that a grandfather reads out to his grandchildren at bedtime. Grandpa's style of telling the tale and the child's own imagination fashion the characters in such a way that they no longer exactly resemble the ones printed over the pages of the book. Similar was the case with these floats that could not be pinned down to the originals. The larger vehicles were finding it immensely difficult to maneuver their way through such a chaos. Many of the participants kept going round and round around the same roundabouts till they went crazy. Many were forced to take longer routes to get on to the roads just across the dividers. Then the fiendish fuel efficiency of these vehicles tripped in, making their chances of winning the contest not only slim but size-zero. The contestants could be seen fuming and fretting as they pushed their vehicles which refused to budge from their place. Some of them were being towed away by the traffic policeman with the challans pasted on their windshields. But there was a mechanical device that did not occupy much space on the road and even if stuck in a jam, was capable of utilizing even a small gap between two vehicles to make its way out. Its rider did not have to run it for long distances to get on the desired route. She simply had to lift its lightweight body over the dividers. As for its mileage, well, with its rider using manpower quite often, its petrol tank very rarely needed refilling.

As Rita entered the precincts of the Panjab University, she headed straight for the Gandhi Bhavan building famous for Gandhian and peace studies and surrounded by water on three sides.

Rita and her mechanical companion were already wobbly with the hard labour of the day. Fatigue had so overpowered Rita that she hoped only to reach the end of her journey; whether she got hold of any booty or not did not bother her. In such a dazed state she did not realize when she crashed through the ribbon of the finishing line at the Gandhi Bhavan. It was a huge round of applause from the crowd that made her conscious of her success. Some volunteers were dragged quite a few yards as they tried to bring Rita and her moped to a halt. Rita was ecstatic as she shared the dais with the chief guest and the president of the organizing committee who garlanded her and presented to her a small trunk which contained the winner's trophy and a cheque. One of the sponsors even signed her for the advertisement campaign of a two-wheeler his company was about to launch in the market. Cameras flashed at Rita, blinding her for some time as she posed confidently beside her lucky charm—her moped. Journalists jostled past each other to ask her just one question over and over again, "How did you manage to win the Treasure Hunt riding so humble a vehicle?" "I think it is the spirit of Chandigarh that I have imbibed in me that helped me win the contest. Unlike India's historical cities, it has not received much by way of a legacy and so have I," she declaimed looking affectionately at her moped. "The city is free from the baggage of the past and has only a present and a future to look forward to and so do I. It has only its own self to rely on and so do I."

Sahil, Ronnie and Aadi had somehow managed to get hold of the last cue-card of the contest. Ronnie had very carefully underlined the key words on the card which according to him were, 'where they all fight,' 'bright,' 'peace' and 'water.' The trio had never quite exercised their brains so that now when they were compelled to do so, their brains were rather upset with the workout. "I know of a place where they regularly fight," Aadi screamed as if struck by lightning. Sahil and Ronnie looked at him with great expectations. "Of course it points towards one of the discotheques in the city; which one, we will shortly figure out," cried out Aadi. Sahil and Ronnie gave him a puzzled look but he explained to them very patiently that discotheques are a favorite hangout for boys and girls to get drunk and create a ruckus. Ronnie was quick to follow the suggestion made by Aadi. "Yes, of course, 'bright' refers to the dazzling lights at the discos and 'peace' to the peacekeepers, that is, the bouncers who keep flexing their muscles to maintain order at these places," he said patting himself for so intelligent an idea. Following the same line of thought, Sahil also put in his two pence, "The reference to water then must stand for the pool that the bouncers use, to throw a real nasty fellow in."

As Rita was riding back home carrying her treasure with her, a group of three boys could be seen hunting for the exact discotheque from among the several located along the Madhya Marg.

One Last Day

The coordinator was busy. He was examining the rehearsals for the grand finale. His sharp eyes watched each detail of every item that was to be staged before the curtains were finally drawn over. The orchestra could be seen fine tuning each instrument, the singers could be spotted vying with each other to occupy the position at the centre and the dancers could be observed sweating it out on the stage. The coordinator paused in front of the dance troupe.

"Hey you", he shouted all of a sudden interrupting the rehearsal.

"The one at the back in blue", he pointed at one of the dancers.

"Me?" asked the one in blue.

"Ya, you, what's your name?" he enquired making an ugly expression.

"Mahesh," he answered.

"Yeah Mahesh, why don't you come out? Yeah come out and leave the stage instantly." He shouted, much to the annoyance of the troupe members.

"And why must he leave? Can't you see he is the best dancer we have?" Now it was the turn of the troupe members to shout.

"What I can see is that his dance steps least synchronize with the rest of you. Synchronization being the most fundamental component for any show to be a success, those who fail to synchronize have no business to be on the stage."

Hearing this Mahesh began climbing down the stage and left the hall banging the door behind him so hard that it almost broke.

"And now if the troupe would please carry on with the rehearsals", the coordinator spoke tersely and moved on to examine the rest of the items. Cursing the sullen coordinator the troupe began to rearrange itself on the stage sans the dancer in blue.

The last day was slowly slipping into history. The sunrays were keeping their hold tight over the day; still it was slipping from their grip.

"Look, look, Ladies and Gentlemen, we had already predicted long back that this would happen. End of Solar days from tomorrow onwards, forever and ever." The panel of experts was visibly perplexed at having to answer the same question over and over again at the press conference.

"The rate at which he was burning his hydrogen fuel, he had to run out of it," lamented the panel.

"So is it official. Is the word final? Do we print tomorrow what you pronounce—'The End'".

"Which paper do you represent?" enquired the panel.

"The Daybreak", he replied.

"Then my friend, give my sincere regards to your head and tell him that his paper would be the first one to bear the brunt of The End. Read my lips 'The End'".

The hall resounded with the shaky laughter of all media persons except for the one representing 'The Daybreak'. It was shaky for everyone feared the inching end and it was laughter because it sounded like one. It always is a relief when someone else is going to be the first one to face something so tragic.

"Calm down, calm down, Ladies and Gentlemen," shouted the panel.

"So, tomorrow onwards when the sun passes from the red giant phase to tiny white dwarf star to finally an invisible black dwarf star stage, curtains will be drawn over the celestial drama of darkness and light, forever and ever."

They had been lying in the ditch since the previous night. Both of them tried to help each other out of it but they kept slipping into it.

"This, isn't this, this . . . ."stammered the tippler.

"This, what this?" the other tippler asked.

"This is the last time we are going to cut a sorry figure across and feel embarrassed", he said.

"Why, are we going to go dry from tomorrow?" the other enquired.

"Dry! My foot! Idiot, this being the last day, we are going to have perpetual darkness from this coming night onwards. And with perpetual darkness comes perpetual flow and a perpetual night life", the tippler remarked.

"Oh my God. So what we are going to live through is an eternal night, an uninterrupted darkness! But, where are all the days going to go?" spoke the tippler, his eyes widening with the shock.

"I know. But I'll let you know only if you promise not to tell anyone else."

"I promise."

"My wife, it's my wife who's going to steal them away and put them in her purse."

"Her purse?"

"Yup, her purse. Do we ever get to see again anything that lands up in her purse?"

"But, isn't the size of the purse too small to carry them all?" the tippler scratched his head.

"Size! My foot! It's Nanotechnology, you wouldn't understand."

The tipplers were quiet for sometime. Finding the calm quiet disquieting, one of them spoke,

"The world is going to witness change and we have still not found a ladder long enough to reach up to the tent above."

"But why do you want to reach up", queried the other.

"To plug the hole in the tent stupid. Maybe we could take a patch and stitch it up there."

"Yeah! But where would you find the fabric similar to the one used for the tent."

"I don't know. But I like the tent. It's silky black and the one who has embroidered shining stars over it has done a skilful job."

"Yeah, but it's kind of tricky."

"Tricky, what tricky?"

"The fibre. Can't you see it changes colours. It's black at night and turns blue by the morning."

The planets had been circumambulating the sun, worshipping the holy fire that burnt ceaselessly in the heart of the universe. Fire that empowered their motion. Motion that was life. Their gait lacked the agility with which they had been going around ever since they came into being. Now they dragged their feet in an unsteady saunter. Had all their worship come to a naught? Was what they revered as eternal actually ephemeral? They panted for breath and smacked their dry lips and looked ahead at the miles yet not travelled. Perhaps the distance travelled so far was all that was to be travelled. But the Moon, the natural satellite of the earth, was silent.

"Come on, come up with some ideas. Now I can't let the 'Zodiac Signs' column to go empty", an ostensibly exasperated editor was pestering the renowned astrologer who made predictions for the column.

"But how could I be expected to make predictions when all the planets are coming to a screeching halt", the astrologer replied.

"I can't risk my business you see. That tiny small column is the only reason why a majority of people subscribe to our paper."

"But the sun and its planets are no longer a reliable system to base my predictions on."

"Then go, look for some other system, some more reliable mechanism that could be trusted with the fate of human beings, my subscribers who keep me in business," pleaded the editor.

Raghu lay with his back resting over the lush green cushioning grass gazing at the sky. Everything appeared so normal, so tranquil. There was nothing in the air that suggested that it was the last time it was going to be normal. He switched on the tiny radio he carried with him hoping to soothe his senses with a melancholic melody. But it was not a melody but the crooning of the panel of experts that was waiting to be heard.

"We assure the general public that our expert team is going to put up a huge apparatus up there in the sky to create the illusion of the day, something like a huge bulb that would run on the mystery fuel we have mined from outer space. For those missing the sun still, we have made arrangements for huge cutouts of the sun to be placed on rooftops of houses located in the eastern direction".

Raghu turned the radio off. "A substitute for the sun?" he moaned. "The sun whose rays tiptoe their way to the sleeping earth, that do not fall harshly over the tender flowers, birds, insects and animals that still have their eyes heavy with the dreams of the past night. The sun that wakes up the earth so softly, so lovingly each morning, and travelling slowly its distance across the sky sharpens his glare and then with the same softness that it comes, takes leave of her so she may refresh herself with a good night's sleep. Sun that always leaves with a promise on his lips of meeting her again the next day." Raghu closed his eyes. Perhaps the barefooted from the Himalayas was not wrong at all. He should have heeded his advice. "I must seek to the light inside. Hope it's not too late," he spoke to himself. He lay in that position; for how long he himself did not know. But something startled him. He opened his eyes. It was a thumping sound. He looked around. There at some distance he could make out the figure of a man who was dancing. Raghu smiled and lay back shutting his eyes. "I envy people who can really afford to be weird in such tumultuous times." He lay quietly but there was some disturbance brewing up among the blades of grass. It was the dew drops.

"Oh how could they pronounce the end over the radio when we are still not decided over our origin", they lamented.

"I insist we are tears that the night sheds", said one of the dew drops.

"No, no we are what fairies sweat", said another.

"Are you mad? Don't you know we are the elixir drops that trickle", argued yet another.

"I object. We are the pearls that bedeck each morning our waking queen", a dew drop objected. And so the dewdrops kept arguing causing quite a ruffle among the blades of grass. But the Moon only pulled a long face and was silent.

Roma was concentrating hard over the crystal ball for the slightest glimpse of events of astronomical proportions but the view was perhaps beyond her focus. As the furrows over her forehead deepened, those around her urged,

"Once more Roma, once more. You are our last hope." Roma tried hard, then harder as others waited with baited breath.

"There, there", she screamed breaking the silence all of a sudden, "he's trying, he's trying hard to dispel her. She! She is not relenting. She is not fighting either. She is just sitting pretty and making her presence felt with her charms and that's enough to cause all the trouble. But he, Oh he is fighting like a hero." The other's edged closer.

"Who is the He you are referring to?" asked a squeaky voice.

"The SUN", Roma shouted.

"And this She?" interrogated a shrill one.

"The Darkness", Roma replied.

"We denounce you, your apparatus and your explanation", the feminists proclaimed getting up from their chairs and throwing up their hands in the air. Roma lay frozen in her chair.

"The Hero, the light of the world, one who is to be revered, the SUN becomes He in the masculine gender and darkness, the root cause of all trouble, the one whose mere presence spells trouble, the one synonymous with ignorance, the one who is to be abhorred, becomes the She in the feminine gender", declaimed a robust feminist standing on a chair.

"How could you Roma, how could you", shrieked the others.

Roma was too dumbfounded to make a reply. Nevertheless she tried, "Please calm down dear friends. If at all anyone is at fault then it is not I but the syntax of the language. Please accept my apologies. I swear to make gender neutral statements."

But it was not before several gallons of cold water had flown down the sleek gullets that the temperature in Roma's room was reduced to normal, bearable degrees of Fahrenheit.

The morning bells at the temple wore a deserted look. They had been heralding the dawning of the day since they had been hung there at the threshold of the temple. The cheerfulness with which they had always chimed the divine element of the morning into the hearts of the mortals was gone. They looked with suspicion at the pujari each time he passed by. Was he having second thoughts at removing them and placing them permanently in the store house at the back of the temple? Oh how bitterly they detested being there in the dark dingy dusty room, lying lifeless among the rest of the junk. But the pujari was not entirely to be blamed. After all what use were Morning Bells without a morning. But what of the bond they had formed with young Neha? Each morning the bells had watched Neha jump high, higher trying to reach the bells. They had watched her fall and bruise her knees. Each morning they had watched her grandpa lift her high to ring the bells. Each morning they had seen the joy that enraptured Neha for having been able to ring the bells.

"Would we never see Neha grow up and reach her hands to ring us", the bells were sad, sonorous sad.

"Morning bells are supposed to usher morning into the world and with vanishing of days wouldn't we lose our identity? But where do we go to lodge our grievance? We, who have been condemned to the threshold of the temple, we who by evening might be shoved into the abominable storehouse." So much of phenomenal proportions was going on around the universe but the Moon was silent.

"We appreciate your attempts at replacing the fading sun. But what arrangements have you made for the phase when the sun in the process of becoming a giant red star will grow brighter and hotter, melting the earth's polar ice caps and turning the oceans to steam leaving us to die in the stifling heat?" Hoping to unnerve the panel of experts with her knowledge the smart woman reporter was herself surprised when the panel gave her an all—knowing smile. She recalled having seen a similar one carved over a statue of Buddha. The imitation was nearly as good as the original.

"Yes, we are prepared for any exigency of the sort you just mentioned. In addition to the curtain we will be using our 7X4 formula to tackle the situation", the panel replied softly.

"7X4 formula! What is this 7X4 formula?" chorused the entire media jam packed in the hall.

"Seven stands for the seven continents and four for each of the four directions. Four men from each continent will be so stationed at the polar ice caps and along the coasts so as to prevent any melting and boiling of caps and oceans respectively", the panel answered with its smile intact.

Media persons looked at each other in disbelief, then scratched their heads and were still scratching when one of them too haunted by the spirit of enquiry asked, "Men? Were men ever capable of such a feat?" The panel again gave its imitation of all knowing smile and clearing its throat replied,

"Dear friends, these are going to be no ordinary men. These will be the ones who top the lists of Icy Cold Men of their respective continents."

"Icy cold!" they again chorused.

"Yes icy cold, almost frozen. Men who have not an iota of emotion left in them. Men who are devoid of any warmth, of love, of kindness. Men who are cold enough to calculate their profits in another man's misery. Men whose heart serves the single purpose of pumping blood. Such men of rare distinction while serving as giant refrigerators will emit such strong icy vibes that nothing around would melt or boil."

The panel had not even finished speaking when feminists began rushing to the streets to protest against the discrimination, for having been ignored representation in the 7X4 formula. After all women were equally capable of being icy and cold.

"But comrade, a perpetual night, now doesn't that translate into perpetual embarrassment for falling into ditches", the tippler was trying to do some coherent thinking.

"And who on earth ever told you that falling into ditches is embarrassing?" the other tippler stared at his companion and then continued, "My dear, it is being caught lying in the ditch that is embarrassing." Saying this he started crying and the other sensing it to be the liquor test of camaraderie joined in, wailing even louder. But his questioning spirit did not seem to lose hold over him.

"Now if I may interrupt? Why are we crying?"

"Comrade, the rising sun always signaled to us that it was time to leave. Now with end of days who'll tell us that it's time to leave the ditches. Buddy, come tomorrow and we will serve a life sentence right here in the ditches." Loud, heart-rending wails of the two tipplers could be heard far and wide.

Young children of Sunflower Public school were the saddest for only a few days ago they had prepared button buddies cut in the shape of sunflowers to wear over their uniforms and now the class teacher was asking them to remove them and throw them into the garbage bin.

"The sunflower is no longer going to remain the logo of our school. In fact the name of the school is also going to be changed. Madam Principal will make an announcement to this effect tomorrow at the assembly", she was explaining to the class.

Palaash looked at his button buddy tied fast over his shirt. He had spent an entire evening trying to make it, resisting the temptation of playing cricket with his friends. That precious button buddy was going to land up in the garbage bin! Tears rolled down Pallavi's plump cheeks as she began removing it from her tunic. How could she forget the pains she took in arranging petals over petals of glaze paper even as the glue kept sticking with her fingers, her face, her dress, her hair, her table and her pencil box? These flowers of 'Sunflower Public School' had withered much before the sunset.

"And now if you have all thrown away your button buddies, take out your books and make corrections with your pencils." The teacher began with the day's lesson. "Yes, here, turn to page number 10, first line of the second paragraph that says 'With each sunrise the day dawns, with each sunset night creeps in.' Now cancel this line with your pencils and in its place write down, 'When the Bulb is switched on there is light, when the Bulb is switched off there is no light.' Palaash at the last bench, hope you are making the necessary corrections." Palaash nodded when in fact he was busy hiding his button buddy in his left shoe.

"But I have a question to ask before you draw the curtains." Someone was heard shouting from the back. Everyone looked in the direction from where the voice was heard and noticed a shabby creature, his hair unkempt, his attire ill-fitting, but one whose eyes carried a spark quite unmatched.

"Go ahead", the panel spoke tersely.

"Will your bulb also manage to make a splash of colours across the sky?"

"Now, what on earth do you need a splash for?" The panel was perplexed. Now a small splash of colours across the table with the aid of a prism is a reasonable proposition but a giant one right across the sky is something quite unreasonable to ask for. The imitation of the smile that the panel had been managing for so long fell all of a sudden into the glasses of water kept over their table and falling thus made a slight spray much to the amusement of the eyes behind the lens. Imitations are after all imitations—unreliable substitutes for the real.

"Don't you realize that I being a poet the splash is my inspiration. And the sun that makes the splash possible is the greatest of all inspirations."

"Look here, it's something as simple as tuning your taste buds to relish boiled food sans spices. Slowly but surely you'll start finding inspiration in our bulb and an imitation of the splash that we'll try to form across the wall of your house."

"You want me to look for inspiration in bulbs, in imitations? Bulbs that make one aspire for brighter bulbs, imitations that make one settle at less than the real?"

Saying this, the creature left the hall to the great relief of the panel. No formula can ever be comprehensive enough to accommodate the poet and his woes.

It was noon and the sun was overhead. Raghu decided to get up and move to a shady spot under the tree. On getting up he noticed that the dancer was still dancing. Raghu kept looking at the dancer for long. He tried to figure out what type of dance the dancer was dancing but found that it was difficult to classify it. But one thing that Raghu was sure of was that it was a dance that had its origin in the dancer. Each movement had a spontaneity of its own. The dancer seemed not as concerned with the movements of the dance as with its enjoyment. He kept his eyes closed, oblivious of the world around him. He seemed to be lost. Lost in the joy that his dancing gave. Raghu noticed that each dance movement was full of energy—Energy that creates, energy that destroys, energy that re-creates. Raghu decided to join the dancer, for getting lost in the joy of a moment was an idea that appealed to him more than worrying over the concerns of past, present or future.

Darkness! Oh for so long she had been lurking in the corners. Now, now was the time to occupy the centre stage. She got up from her cosmic chair and took a step forward. Then as she was about to lift her next foot she realized it had got stuck. She gave a loud cry, then looked down at her jammed foot. There, chained tightly to her foot was Fear—the scary. It was the first time she noticed him in so many years. He had indeed attained enormous proportions. She tried to pull her foot but could not, for he was sleeping peacefully, all curled up at her foot. She tried to shake him out of his slumber, but he did not wake up. Now she was indignant. She stomped the other foot hard at him. Now he was hurt. Keeping his eyes shut he began to speak dreamily,

"Her Highness, as her highness already knows that it is in sleeping here that I awake in the deep recesses of the minds of life forms, crippling them and leading them to your court. My regrets for having been unable to lead the golden one to your presence-the one who has no parallel in the whole universe, the one who is not the slave but the master of his mind." Her

Highness could not contain her hatred for the sleeper who made her limp and drag herself. How hard had she always tried to prove that there was no alternative to her, that she was the supreme power. And Sun, that flaming spoilsport had managed to show everyone that the alternative was actually possible. But now she was convinced that her time was come and move she must to conquer and annex. And for how long could she resist her invocation by her numerous worshippers over the earth who dabbed her lips to keep them blazing like embers. But the Moon, the shiny lamp that made lovers speak their heart out was in no mood to speak even from its voice box and was silent.

Twenty four wheels and seven horses screeched and halted. The golden chariot had got stuck. You could tell from the condition of the chariot that it had been through a battle that had not ceased for a single moment. Perhaps, even the chariot builder had not fathomed while carving flowers, their petals, creepers and leaves over the chariot that it was going to fight a battle that demanded tougher motifs, a battle that no one ever could fight, a battle that was unending. The occupant of the golden chariot reclined in meditative silence. Memories came floating of the times when he had first set out into the bogging darkness and finding no ray of light had resolved to exude light and warmth from within and reach out to the numerous frozen rocky barren souls. But battles don't end at the point where the chariot gets stuck, nor even at the point where the chariot breaks and ceases.

The Moon was silent. It was silent not because it didn't have anything to say but because no one had bothered to ask for its opinion. The moon knew it wouldn't have a single phase to show to the world without the sun. It had taken the sun's light for granted. Now it would have to do without light even on full moon nights. But more than its phases, the Moon was worried about the old woman spinning the wheel.

"Spinning by the dark would only make her eyesight worse. And God knows how much more spinning remains to be done."